The Case of
the Floating Crime

Cautiously Nancy followed the curve of the ship's upper deck. She heard no sound, not even footsteps. Was Conner waiting for her just around the curve? she wondered, holding her breath.

Eventually she reached the starboard side. Listening intently for sounds ahead of her, she didn't hear the footsteps behind her until it was too late.

Before she could turn, Nancy felt a hard push in the middle of her back. She tried to grab the railing, but her fingers slipped off the slick painted wood.

In a second she had toppled over the side, plunging down toward the dark, cold waters of the Muskoka River!

Nancy Drew
Mystery Stories

Available from MINSTREL Books

NANCY DREW MYSTERY STORIES®

120

NANCY DREW®

THE CASE OF THE FLOATING CRIME

CAROLYN KEENE

A MINSTREL® BOOK

Published by POCKET BOOKS
New York   London   Toronto   Sydney   Singapore

This book is a work of fiction. Names, characters, places, and incidents are products of the author's imagination or are used fictitiously. Any resemblance to actual events or locales or persons, living or dead, is entirely coincidental.

A MINSTREL PAPERBACK *ORIGINAL*

 A Minstrel Book published by
POCKET BOOKS, a division of Simon & Schuster Inc.
1230 Avenue of the Americas, New York, NY 10020

Copyright © 1994 by Simon & Schuster Inc.

Produced by Mega-Books of New York, Inc.

All rights reserved, including the right to reproduce this book or portions thereof in any form whatsoever. For information address Pocket Books, 1230 Avenue of the Americas, New York, NY 10020

ISBN: 0-671-87203-6

First Minstrel Books printing August 1994

10 9 8 7 6 5 4

NANCY DREW, NANCY DREW MYSTERY STORIES, A MINSTREL BOOK and colophon are registered trademarks of Simon & Schuster Inc.

Cover art by Aleta Jenks

Printed in the U.S.A.

Contents

THE CASE OF THE
FLOATING CRIME

1

A Face in the Window

"Why are we picking up Bess so early? I thought she worked until five on Saturdays," George Fayne asked her friend Nancy Drew.

Nancy skillfully eased her blue Mustang into a narrow space in the Riverside Hospital parking lot. "Bess has to leave early to go to a meeting," Nancy explained as she got out and closed the car door. Her reddish blond hair brushed the collar of her turquoise pullover. "And she said she wanted to talk to us first."

"Oh, no," George groaned, unfolding her tall body out of the car. "Not one of Bess's goofy projects." Sliding her sunglasses on top of her head, she followed Nancy up the hospital steps.

The sharp smell of hospital disinfectant filled their noses as they walked across the large, brightly decorated reception area. "Where is the

1

volunteer office, please?" Nancy asked the man who sat at the information desk.

"Just follow the blue line," he said, pointing down over the side of the desk. Stripes of blue, red, yellow, and green were painted on the floor, each one leading to a different wing of the hospital.

Nancy and George followed the blue stripe to the North Wing. Noticing a door marked Volunteer Office, Nancy pushed it open.

"Great! You found me." Bess Marvin jumped up from her chair, her long straw blond hair bouncing.

Over her pale yellow dress she wore a long pink- and white-striped tunic with full sleeves pushed up to her elbows. Nancy recognized the tunic as the uniform of the candy stripers, a group of teenage boys and girls who donated several hours each week to help at the hospital.

Candy stripers delivered flowers and mail, assisted patients who needed help eating, and played with the children in the pediatric wards. Once in a while, they got to rock the newborn babies—one of Bess's favorite duties.

"Quick, let's go," Bess said. She darted past Nancy and George and bustled out the door. "Maria's waiting."

"Who's Maria?" George asked, hurrying along with Bess. Although the two girls were cousins, they were total opposites—George was dark-haired, slim, and athletic, while Bess was blond and ever so slightly plump.

"She's a new friend I met here," Bess answered. "I've been trying to cheer her up—she's been kind of moody lately. I don't know what's bothering her. Nancy, you're the detective—maybe you can find out."

The girls followed Bess down the hall and around the corner to a small lunchroom that was equipped with a refrigerator, vending machines, two microwave ovens, and chairs and tables.

Bess headed for a window table, where a pretty, dark-haired girl was sitting. She smiled warmly when she saw Bess.

Bess quickly introduced the girls to one another. "I see you're a candy striper, too," Nancy said to Maria, nodding at the girl's striped top.

"Yes. It was sort of expected of me, but I do love it," Maria said, her dark brown eyes lighting up.

"Maria's father is Dr. Armando Diaz," Bess explained. "He's one of the most important doctors here at Riverside."

"Shhh, Bess," Maria said, looking around. "I told you, we don't need to broadcast that. I don't want to be treated any differently than anyone else at work."

On the table in front of Maria sat a half-eaten slice of apple pie. George eyed it hungrily. "That looks good. Where'd you get it?" she asked Maria.

"From the machines," Maria said, pointing.

George dug into her pocket for some coins and headed for the vending machine. "Can I get you anything, Nancy? Bess?"

"Sure, I'll have a piece," Nancy replied, pulling out a chair and sitting down.

"None for me," Bess called over to George. "It'll be swimsuit weather in less than a month, and I have to lose five pounds by then."

"But, Bess, you didn't have any lunch today," Maria reminded her, looking concerned. "You shouldn't starve yourself. That's not a healthy way to lose weight."

"If you really want to lose weight, why don't you start exercising a little?" George remarked, returning to the table with two plates of pie.

"That's easy for *you* to say—you like sports," Bess complained.

Nancy heard the hurt in Bess's voice and decided to change the subject. "So what did you want to talk about?" she asked Bess gently.

Bess's mood changed almost instantly. "This is so exciting, I know you'll want to do it."

"We will?" George said. "Do what?"

"Be a *Heartliner* hostess!" Bess announced. "Tell them, Maria."

"As you probably know, the *Heartliner* is docking tomorrow in River Heights," Maria began.

"Oh, yes," Nancy said. "I've been reading the articles about it in the paper. It's not often that a medical missionary ship comes to town."

"The ship sails to Central and South America twice a year, staying three months each trip," Maria explained. "She takes medical supplies and doctors and nurses to areas that don't have any medical help at all otherwise."

"It's wonderful!" Bess chimed in. "They help all these people, especially little children. It's like a real hospital, only on a ship."

"My dad is chief of staff during the ship's tours," Maria said, "and it was his idea to bring the *Heartliner* here. The people of River Heights have donated lots of money over the years. Now they'll be able to see her for themselves."

"What's a *Heartliner* hostess?" Nancy asked.

"While the ship is here, several schools will take field trips on board," Maria said.

"The kids will love it!" Bess interrupted. "They'll really get to see how a hospital works."

"*Heartliner* staff members will give eye tests and hearing tests to the students and demonstrate medical procedures," Maria went on quietly. "They'll show how the different wards and clinics on ship operate—that sort of thing."

Nancy noticed that Maria seemed distracted and a little sad as she talked, even though she appeared to be genuinely interested in the ship and proud of her father's role on it.

"The hostesses and hosts will help lead the students around, give tours, and help with demonstrations," Bess broke in enthusiastically. "All of us candy stripers were asked to be hostesses

5

and hosts, but two girls had to bow out this morning, so we want you to fill in for them. Oh, please say you'll do it! It will be so much fun—a once-in-a-lifetime experience."

"You don't have to sell me," Nancy said. "It sounds wonderful. I'd love to."

"Me, too," George said, licking her fork.

"Oh, good." Bess sighed with relief. "Because I already signed you up. So hurry up and finish that stupid pie—we're all due at a meeting at Maria's house in twenty minutes!"

"Bess!" Nancy protested, gulping down a bite.

Twenty minutes later Nancy swung her car around a curve heading to the Diazes' house. "Turn left at the next stop sign," Maria instructed her from the front passenger seat.

"Who'll be at this meeting?" George asked from the backseat.

"There are eight hostesses and six hosts. Oh, and the Diazes, of course," said Bess, seated beside George. "Nancy, your dad may know Maria's mother—she's a lawyer, just like he is."

"Mr. Clayton will probably be there," Maria added. "He's the chairman of the *Heartliner*'s board of directors."

"Will Sara Lawson be there, Maria?" Bess asked with dread in her voice.

"Who's she?" Nancy asked.

"She's director of the *Heartliner* nursing staff,"

Maria explained. "And when the ship is docked, she supervises the candy stripers."

"I've only had to deal with her a couple of times, but that was enough." Bess shivered. "She's famous for her mean temper. All the candy stripers are afraid of her."

"Hmmm," George muttered. "I can't wait."

"And Pepe Morales will be there!" Bess added. Nancy could hear her friend's mood brighten instantly.

"I read about him in one of the newspaper articles," Nancy said. "The boy from Argentina?"

"Right," Bess said, grinning. "He almost died from some sort of fever, and the staff of the *Heartliner* saved his life. Now he's coming to live with the Diazes so he can go to Riverview College and study to be a doctor. I saw his photo— he's really cute. Aren't you excited, Maria?"

Maria looked out of the window at the passing lawns and houses. "I guess so," she said in a distant tone of voice.

Nancy caught Bess's eye in her rearview mirror. Bess's pointed gaze clearly said, See what I mean? Nancy nodded briefly, wondering to herself what was bothering Bess's new friend.

The drive leading to the Diaz home was lined with crab apple trees in full flower. Nancy pulled into the parking area at the side of the large, grand Tudor-style house.

Mrs. Diaz, a petite woman in a red suit, met the girls at the door. "The meeting hasn't started yet," she said, "because we're waiting for my husband to bring Pepe from the airport. Come on, you all can help me get the refreshments ready." She led them down the hall to the back of the house.

The kitchen was huge, with glistening slate counters and white cabinets. Six windows flooded the room with light. A couple of trays of appetizers—tiny wedges of pizza and sausages wrapped in flaky pastry—were laid out on an island counter. Bess leaned over the trays, staring hungrily with her hands behind her back.

Maria walked into a small pantry off to the side. Nancy watched her reach for a package of party napkins on a high shelf. As the cellophane wrapping broke, bright orange and pink napkins fluttered down to the floor.

"Ahhh!" Maria wailed. Instead of picking up the napkins, she sank down on a nearby step stool and covered her face with her hands.

Nancy frowned. Maria's reaction was too strong for just a package of spilled napkins, she decided, and she started toward the pantry. Bess beat her there. "Maria, what is it?" Bess murmured, kneeling down by her friend.

"No, please, I can't talk about it," Maria said, her voice quavering.

"Maria, I know we've just met," Nancy said gently, "but if there's anything we can do—"

"I told Nancy and George that you've been upset lately," Bess blurted out. "I know they'll be happy to help—we all will. Nancy is really good at tracking down answers and solving problems, and we're all good listeners."

"I didn't want anyone to see me like this. It's just—" Maria darted a worried glance over Bess's shoulder toward the kitchen. "I'm so worried about Dad," she admitted in a low voice. "He's been acting crazy lately. Half the time he's yelling at me and Mom for no reason—he's never done that before. The rest of the time he looks like he's lost his best friend."

"Maybe he's anxious about the *Heartliner*'s visit," Nancy suggested. "With the student tours and everything, he could be concerned about everything going smoothly. Have you talked to your mother about it?"

Maria looked at Nancy and her dark eyes were sad. "I mentioned it to Mom, and she says it's stress from his job, but I think it's more than that, and I want to help him. Do you really think we can find out what it is?"

"We sure can try," Nancy said.

"If Nancy says she'll help, the mystery's practically solved already," Bess said loyally.

Maria wiped her eyes and smiled weakly. "Thank you. Bess said you were good friends, and she's right."

Bess and Nancy helped Maria gather up the napkins and returned to the main kitchen. Nancy

9

noticed that a frown still crumpled Maria's forehead as she picked up the pizza tray.

Maria left the kitchen, carrying her tray down a short hall. George followed her with a coffeepot and a pitcher of juice. Bess carried out a plate of cookies, while Mrs. Diaz brought up the rear with the tray of sausage rolls.

Left alone, Nancy went to the refrigerator to fill an ice bucket. Placing it under the dispenser in the door, she watched the cubes fall.

Suddenly the back of Nancy's neck tingled. She had a creepy feeling that someone else was there with her.

She wheeled around toward the window—and looked straight into a pair of large green eyes. Just outside stood a man she'd never seen before, staring at her intently!

2

Someone Is Lying

The stranger's head dropped out of sight immediately, but not before Nancy had gotten a good look at him. She noticed that he had curly dark blond hair, a droopy light brown mustache, and those huge, startled green eyes.

Springing to the kitchen door, Nancy threw it open and looked outside. She saw the man dashing across the lawn, dressed in jeans and a gray windbreaker.

Nancy stepped out onto the flagstone terrace. "Hey, you there," she called out. "Stop!"

The man only ran faster. He must be up to no good, or he wouldn't keep running, Nancy thought.

Sprinting, she followed him at a safe distance, trying to stay concealed. She slipped around a tall blue spruce tree, then crouched behind a lush lilac bush.

The stranger's thin figure disappeared around the corner of the garden shed. Nancy sidled slowly along the building, holding her breath.

She swung around the back of the shed just in time to see the man disappear over a high stone wall. Running to the wall, she took a flying leap and just barely grabbed the top, hanging there by her fingertips. With great exertion, she pulled herself up and peered over the wall. She saw nothing on the other side but dense woods.

Frustrated, Nancy dropped back to the ground, brushed herself off, and jogged back to the house. As she ran, she mentally reviewed the man's description so she wouldn't forget any detail.

When she came in the kitchen door, Bess was waiting for her. "Where have you been?" Bess whispered. Without waiting for an answer, she grabbed Nancy's arm. "Come on—Pepe's here!"

Bess dragged Nancy to the sun room, where the meeting was being held. "Ooooh, there he is," Bess whispered, poking Nancy in the ribs. Nancy followed Bess's gaze to Pepe Morales, sitting on a sofa beside Mrs. Diaz. Casually dressed in jeans and a blue- and white-striped shirt, he had dark brown, almost black eyes, dazzling white teeth, and golden skin. His hair was black and wavy, with a few long curls brushing his forehead.

"Ah," Francesca Diaz said as she spotted Bess

and Nancy, "you're back. We can start now." She motioned for them to join George on the long window seat, piled high with blue and yellow floral pillows.

In a whisper, Nancy told Bess and George about the man she'd seen peeking in the Diazes' kitchen window. "How creepy!" Bess said, shivering.

"What do you suppose he wanted?" George wondered. "What was he looking for?"

"Or who?" Nancy added.

Nancy glanced around the sun room. Late afternoon sunlight streamed through the tall windows and glinted off the glass coffee table. On the sofa sat Pepe, Mrs. Diaz, and two men in suits and ties. Nancy guessed that the one right next to Mrs. Diaz was Maria's father. His wavy black hair was thinning on top, and his neatly trimmed black beard and mustache were flecked with silver. Nancy noticed that he also had dark circles below his eyes.

Dr. Diaz stood up, clearing his throat. Welcoming everyone, he began introductions. In a semicircle of chairs sat six women dressed in white nurses' uniforms with *Heartliner* embroidered on the pockets. Dr. Diaz introduced them as members of the ship's staff who would help with the school field trips. Scanning their faces, Nancy wondered which one was Sara Lawson.

On the other side of the room, about a dozen

13

teenage boys and girls sat sprawled on the carpet or crowded on one long sofa. Dr. Diaz introduced them as the *Heartliner* hostesses and hosts.

Just then a door chime warbled through the room. It sounded again, then again and again, until it became irritating. Someone was apparently leaning on the doorbell. Everyone turned to look toward the sound.

"We're especially pleased that Pepe is with us," Dr. Diaz was saying. He had to raise his voice over the door chime.

Then the noise stopped. Nancy looked through the sun room door and saw the Diazes' housekeeper pointing the way to the meeting. A tall, bony woman pushed past her and strode into the sun room.

She appeared to be in her forties and wore no makeup or jewelry. Her dark red hair was pulled back tightly and pinned in place, and her eyes were magnified by thick, round eyeglasses. Refusing the chair Dr. Diaz offered her, she leaned against the wall near Nancy and her friends, arms tightly crossed over her chest.

"Sara, we're so glad you made it," Dr. Diaz said to her politely. He turned back to the volunteers. "Many of you already know Sara Lawson, head of the *Heartliner* nursing staff. She will supervise the student field trips.

"When the *Heartliner* sails," Dr. Diaz continued, "it carries a regular staff of about fifty medical personnel and crew members. A small core group of doctors, nurses, and technicians are permanent members of the Riverside Hospital staff and live here when the *Heartliner* is not at sea. We also have rotators—specialists who fly into various ports to volunteer for a few days' work.''

Dr. Diaz paced toward a large rubber tree in a pot in the corner of the room. "You'll be our rotators for the River Heights docking," he continued with a small smile, "and I'm pleased to introduce your chief of staff, Pepe Morales."

Pepe rose from his chair and stood next to Dr. Diaz. *"Buenos días*—hello!" Pepe said, with a merry grin. "I owe my life to the *Heartliner*, so I am lucky to be its spokesperson. I'm glad I can help teach the world about the fine work done by her wonderful staff." His English was good, and Nancy guessed that he enjoyed speaking before a group.

"Thank you, Pepe," Dr. Diaz said. "We're also honored to have Alexander Clayton with us today." He gestured toward the other man on the love seat. "Alex owns Clayton Imports, but more important—for me, at least—he helped found the *Heartliner*, and he's her biggest booster. Alex, would you like to say anything to our River Heights rotators?"

Alexander Clayton stood, dwarfing Dr. Diaz. He was a tall stocky man, handsome, with a thick mane of silver hair and large dark blue eyes.

"Thank you, Armando," Clayton said in a

mellow, deep voice. "There is nothing dearer to my heart than the *Heartliner*. Thanks to Armando and Francesca, the ship's staff, and you volunteers, this will be an exciting week for our city."

Nancy heard a muffled snort explode from Sara Lawson. "Uh-oh, here we go," Bess whispered to Nancy. "I thought she'd been quiet for too long."

Ignoring Nurse Lawson's snort, Mr. Clayton said a few more inspirational words and then sat down. Dr. Diaz rose again. "Sara, could you tell us about the week's activities?" he asked.

With a firm nod, the red-haired nurse straightened up and spoke in a clipped, no-nonsense tone. "The *Heartliner* will dock around eleven o'clock tomorrow morning," she said, concluding her talk. "You volunteers will receive your orientation tour at noon. I'll see you then." With another curt nod, she wheeled and left the room as abruptly as she had entered.

As Dr. Diaz stood up and continued the meeting, Nancy noticed Alexander Clayton slip to his feet and follow Nurse Lawson out into the hall outside the sun room. Curious, Nancy got up and strolled over to the hall doorway to eavesdrop.

"I'm fed up with your attitude, Nurse Lawson," Clayton was whispering fiercely, "and I'm not the only one. We've had several complaints from your staff."

"I don't answer to you," the nurse said crisply.

"Yes, you do, Ms. Lawson," Clayton said. "You report to Dr. Diaz, and Dr. Diaz reports to me."

16

"The *Heartliner* belongs to Riverside Hospital and to the people she helps," Lawson countered, her voice growing louder. "And it's time you stopped using the ship to glorify your own public image. She exists to help those in need, not to make you famous."

"Why, I can't—I don't know what you—That's preposterous," Clayton stammered.

"No, it's not," Lawson insisted shrilly.

As her voice rose in argument, everyone in the meeting was glancing uneasily toward the hallway. Dr. Diaz broke off in midsentence, looking anxious.

"More refreshments, anyone?" Mrs. Diaz asked, standing up. Her voice sounded strangled with embarrassment.

"I know you were responsible for the change in the itinerary on the last mission," Lawson continued loudly in the hallway, shaking a finger in Clayton's face. "We passed by villages that needed help, then docked in cities where *you* could give interviews to the international press—and be photographed with Pepe a million times."

Dr. Diaz stepped quickly to the hallway. The meeting fell into dead silence as everyone listened to the altercation.

"This is not the time to be discussing this, Sara," Dr. Diaz said uneasily, putting his hand on her shoulder.

"No, Armando," Nurse Lawson yelled. "I

won't be quiet any longer. We can't let him take over the ship."

"That's enough," Clayton said, his voice tight with anger. "You're off the *Heartliner* permanently! Effective now!"

Nancy felt someone breathing heavily beside her. She turned to see Maria, her eyes wide as she watched with Nancy.

"You can't fire me," Lawson said, waving her arm wildly. "I answer only to Dr. Diaz."

"Very well." Clayton turned to Maria's father. "Fire her, Armando."

Dr. Diaz's face grew pale. Nancy heard Maria gasp and hold her breath. "Sara," Dr. Diaz pleaded. "Let's go into my study and talk this over privately."

"Think what's best for the *Heartliner*, Armando," Clayton said with a significant look. He turned on his heel and strode to the front door.

Dr. Diaz's shoulders slumped. "You're out, Sara," he said numbly.

A look of betrayal flashed across the nurse's plain face. "Doctor?" she gasped.

Dr. Diaz merely shook his head.

Nurse Lawson's face was flushed with rage. "You won't get away with this, Armando," she hissed. "There have been several incidents recently that make no sense, and you know what I mean. Well, I'm not going to stand by and do nothing. Either the *Heartliner* fulfills her original

18

purpose, or she doesn't sail at all!" With that, Nurse Lawson stormed out the front door herself.

Dr. Diaz stood alone for a moment, staring dully at the carpet. Then he moved stiffly toward the front hall staircase and climbed upstairs without looking back. Brushing past Nancy, Maria ran after him.

The next morning Nancy was awakened by the phone at seven-thirty, a half hour before her alarm was set to go off.

"Nancy? It's Maria. Can you come over here, please? Right now?" The words tumbled through the phone, forcing Nancy to wake up quickly. "I found some papers in my father's study last night that I'd like you to look at."

"Mmmm, sure," Nancy mumbled. "Yes, of course. I'll be there as soon as I can."

Nancy dressed quickly in a dusty rose slim skirt and matching sweater and put on comfortable flats. She knew she'd be doing a lot of walking during the student field trips.

Maria was waiting at her front door when Nancy got there. "My parents and Pepe left for a breakfast meeting," Maria said as she took Nancy straight into Armando Diaz's study. It was a beautiful room, with dark polished wood, soft sleek leather, and hundreds of books.

"After the scene with Nurse Lawson and Alexander Clayton yesterday, I'm convinced that my dad's worries have something to do with the

Heartliner," Maria said. She pointed to several papers spread out on a long table. "So I went through Dad's desk and I found this file." She handed a folder to Nancy. "It doesn't have a label, but it's related to the ship. Look at the weight numbers for the last two cruises."

Nancy studied the papers for almost ten minutes. There was something odd. Then she realized what it was. "Maria," Nancy said. "These papers aren't for two different cruises—both sets are for the same trip."

Maria looked confused. "I don't understand."

Nancy held up two papers. "Look at the dates. One set is signed by your father, and one set is signed by Alexander Clayton, but the numbers on them are very different. There's definitely something fishy here!"

3

A Stranger's Warning

"Two sets of records for the same trip?" Maria repeated. "But why?"

"I don't know," Nancy said. "But look—here are cargo manifests and customs declarations for the four cruises before this." Nancy fished some other papers from the file. "They all have about the same weights, numbers, and cargo listings."

Nancy spread the papers out on the table to compare them. "Here are the two sets of papers for the last cruise. This first set—the one Mr. Clayton signed—is in line with the previous ones. But the set your dad signed shows that the *Heartliner* weighed several tons more on the return trip than she did going out!"

"How could that be?" Maria said. "They never bring anything back to the States."

"Maybe medical equipment?" Nancy suggested.

"No, I don't think so," Maria said. "Sometimes they take a lot of equipment down to Latin America, but they leave it in the villages." She studied the papers, frowning. "Who signed the previous cruise records?" she asked.

"Your dad did," Nancy answered.

"And Alexander Clayton signed one of the sets for the last cruise?" Maria asked.

"Yes." Nancy pointed to his signature.

"Then Nurse Lawson is right." Maria sighed. "Alexander Clayton has taken over the *Heartliner*. Maybe he's trying to bring in another doctor to be chief of staff." She looked up, her dark eyes full of worry. "That would break Dad's heart."

Nancy wondered if that was all there was to it, but she decided not to voice her doubts to Maria until she knew more.

Maria was still staring at the two sets of papers. "The odd one, the heavy one—that was the one signed by Dad," Maria said softly. "There *is* something funny going on, and he seems to be right in the middle of it."

"Don't worry, Maria, we'll figure it out." Nancy gave her new friend a reassuring smile.

Dr. Diaz had a desktop photocopy machine in the large closet of his study. Nancy made copies of all the cruise records, including the two sets for the last trip. Maria tidied up the room.

By the time they had finished, it was after ten

o'clock and time to get to the river for the arrival of the *Heartliner*.

It took them a while to drive across town because the traffic was terrible. Streets were clogged with people walking, biking, and driving. All were headed to the widest point of the Muskoka River, a natural harbor between Riverside Hospital and the warehouses on Front Street.

Nancy and Maria parked three blocks away and walked to the river. Bleachers had been set up along the riverbank. The stands were already full, but Maria led Nancy to a section designated for *Heartliner* volunteers. Looking up, Nancy saw Bess and George wave and point to the seats they'd saved for Nancy and Maria.

"Where have you been?" Bess said excitedly as Nancy and Maria joined them.

"We'll tell you later," Nancy said. "For now, we're going to enjoy the festivities—right, Maria?" Maria smiled gamely.

George stood up and looked toward the speakers. "There's Pepe," she pointed out, as they watched him climb up to the VIP platform. "You're right, Bess. He's one cute guy."

"Why, George," Bess teased her cousin. "If I didn't know better, I'd think you were interested in our amigo from Argentina."

"George, you're blushing," Maria added.

"It's not the first time," Nancy said, laughing, "but it's rare enough."

23

A huge crowd had gathered by now. Nancy had brought a small pair of binoculars with her, and scanning the crowd, she saw all the civic leaders of River Heights and the top staff of Riverside Hospital. She also recognized several newspaper and television reporters in the press pen.

The river was full, too. Dozens of sailboats, yachts, and other small craft were gathered to watch the big ship sail in.

The sounds of a lively mariachi band drifted upriver on the wind, growing louder. Nancy gasped as the ship rounded the bend. The *Heartliner* was huge—four hundred feet long— with freshly painted white sides and decks. Bright-colored streamers and pennants fluttered on ropes strung between the decks. It was a breathtaking sight.

A temporary pontoon dock had been con- structed to reach out to the mighty ship. Slowly and skillfully, the *Heartliner* crew maneuvered the ship up to the dock and then dropped the five-ton anchor into the Muskoka. The crowd of onlookers filled the air with cheers and whistles.

Local leaders gave brief speeches, and then Dr. Diaz addressed the crowd. Nancy noticed Maria's face cloud over as she watched her fa- ther. "Last, but not least, I must express my appreciation to Alexander Clayton for his sup- port," Dr. Diaz said.

Clayton stood and waved to the crowd as the applause rippled across the riverbank.

"Without the work of this dedicated man," Dr. Diaz continued, "we wouldn't have this ship. As most of you know, we are concluding this week with a dinner for him next Friday. We look forward to seeing many of you there. Now I'd like to introduce the *Heartliner*'s ambassador of goodwill, Pepe Morales."

Pepe stood and waved. Nancy noticed that his smile was dazzling even from a distance.

"*Gracias.* You have made me feel so welcome," Pepe said. "I am very happy to be a new citizen of River Heights." The crowd cheered wildly.

"And now I have some exciting news," he said. "I am happy to announce that, for the first time ever, the *Heartliner* is sailing on a medical mission to the Far East. She will be leaving River Heights on Friday night after the banquet."

Over the applause, Nancy heard Maria murmur, "That's odd. Dad never mentioned that at all."

After the speeches, many people settled in on the riverbank for a picnic. Meanwhile, the *Heartliner* hostesses and hosts ran up the gangway—the long ramp connecting the ship to the dock—for an orientation tour led by Dr. Diaz and Pepe. The press followed closely behind, escorted separately by Alexander Clayton.

As the tour moved about the ship, Nancy was fascinated by the *Heartliner*'s layout. An old navy ship, it had been modified to include operating

25

and recovery rooms, labs, examination rooms, a dental clinic, and a pharmacy.

"The hallways—or companionways, as we call them—are painted beige and pale blue," Pepe pointed out. "These colors look cool in the hot tropical countries where the ship docks." Red signs gave directions in both English and Spanish.

Dr. Diaz led the tour into a large classroom with seventy-five school desks. "One of the principal purposes of the *Heartliner* is to teach," he said. "We hold class sessions at every port, teaching local doctors and nurses new and more efficient ways to practice medicine. We also give daily language classes to our staff and crew."

"Local students sometimes serve as trainees in the labs and blood bank," Pepe added. "After the *Heartliner* cured my fever and infection, I signed on. This is where I decided to become a doctor—as a trainee in this room."

The volunteers were led through an adult ward, an intensive care unit, a medical library, a central supply room, and even a chapel. In the children's ward, Bess nudged Nancy to notice the walls, painted with a mural of Noah's ark.

Beds in the hospital wards were suspended on chains, and most of the other furniture was bolted to the wall. Dr. Diaz explained that everything had to be fastened down when they were at sea, in case of rough weather.

Elevators took the group down to the staff and

crew quarters. "As you can see, this is no cruise ship." Pepe grinned, opening a staff cabin.

"Believe it or not," Dr. Diaz added, "four people live in here." The room was very small, with two bunks attached to the walls and two that could be lowered from the ceiling.

The tour ended back in the classroom, where the hostesses and hosts received information about the field trip to be conducted the next morning. They also met the nurses they'd be working with. Nancy, Bess, George, and Maria checked the week's schedule posted on the bulletin board.

"We're working together tomorrow, Nancy," Bess said, "doing vision tests in the eye clinic. Maria, you're going to be in the pharmacy, and George and Pepe will be in the admissions area, helping the nurses with vaccine shots. Ugh."

Nancy and her friends returned to the deck. "I'm going to walk to the hospital to meet Dad," Maria said. "My family's taking Pepe out to lunch." She said goodbye to the girls and headed for the gangway.

"Speaking of food," George said, turning to Nancy and Bess, "isn't the Pizza Palace right around the corner from here?"

"It's that way, on River Lane," Nancy added, pointing. She leaned over the railing, taking in the view. She could see the people picnicking along the river, the now empty bleachers, and the speaker's stand, where the mariachi band was playing a concert.

Then she noticed Dr. Diaz standing by the press tent at the foot of the gangway. Suddenly, she saw a man walking quickly toward the tent.

There was something threatening about the way he was heading right for Maria's father, one hand jammed into his gray jacket pocket. Nancy felt a stab of fear in her stomach. She reached into her tote bag and took out her binoculars.

Nancy fixed her sight on the man hurrying toward the unsuspecting Dr. Diaz. It was the stranger she'd seen at the Diaz home—the man with the blond curly hair and droopy mustache!

"What is it, Nan?" George asked.

Nancy had no time to answer. "Dr. Diaz!" she yelled, but the blaring trumpets of the mariachis drowned her out. Heart pounding, she raced away from her friends and tore down the gangway toward the tent.

As she ran, Nancy kept her eyes fixed on the stranger. The man came up to Dr. Diaz and jabbed his arm forward. He thrust something into the startled doctor's hand and ran off.

Nancy stopped and gasped with relief. She watched Dr. Diaz look at a piece of paper. Then his head jerked up, panic crossing his face.

The doctor stared in the direction the stranger had gone. For a minute Nancy thought Dr. Diaz was going to follow him. Instead, he wadded up

28

the paper and threw it into a trash bin. Then he walked quickly toward Riverside Hospital.

Nancy ran over to the trash bin. A crumpled piece of yellow paper lay atop a jumble of coffee cups, soiled paper napkins, and film boxes. She pulled it out. A chill ran up her spine as she read the message, handwritten in thick black pencil: "I'm not going to let you get away with this. I'll figure it out."

4

A Poisonous Prescription

Nancy shuddered. She knew now that Maria's father was in trouble. Somehow the stranger had found out about it and was threatening Dr. Diaz, maybe even blackmailing him. And she felt sure it had something to do with the two sets of records for the last *Heartliner* cruise.

Bess and George caught up with Nancy just then. "What was that all about, Nancy?" Bess puffed, trying to catch her breath.

Nancy quickly told them about the mysterious stranger passing the note to the doctor. Then she explained what she and Maria had found that morning in Dr. Diaz's study.

George whistled as she read the crumpled note. "This could mean anything," she said cautiously.

"Well, I think it's pretty clear," Bess said. "Maria's dad is doing something that this guy doesn't like. That's why he was peeking in the window yesterday—to spy on Dr. Diaz."

"Yes, but even the stranger doesn't seem to know what's going on exactly," Nancy pointed out. "He wrote, 'I'll figure it out.'"

"Well, we'll just have to figure it out before he does," Bess declared.

Nancy nodded. "Let's get to work. Some of the nurses are still on board, getting ready for the field trips. Could you two interview some of them? Find out what supplies the ship carries back and forth, who runs things on board, and what Nurse Lawson's really like—that sort of thing."

"Will do," George said with a grin and a salute.

After Bess and George went back up the gangway, Nancy looked around, planning her next move. She spotted Alexander Clayton on the *Heartliner*'s forward deck, talking with a group of reporters. Some of them held microphones in front of his face, while others scribbled in notebooks.

Alexander Clayton signed the second set of cruise records, Nancy mused. Maybe I can find out something from him. Reporter Nancy Drew, it's time to investigate! She pulled a small spiral notebook and pen from her tote bag, ran up the gangway, and fell in with the group of reporters.

"Here's one of our *Heartliner* hostesses now," Clayton said, noticing her. "Ms. Drew, isn't it?"

"Yes, it is," Nancy said. "May I join the other

reporters? I'm writing a firsthand account of my experiences this week."

"Of course," he said with a courteous nod. "What would you like to ask?"

Nancy flipped her notebook open. "Could you tell us about the management of the *Heartliner?*"

"What do you mean exactly?" he replied. Nancy thought she saw his shoulders tense.

"As I understand it, Dr. Diaz is the chief of staff, and he is responsible for all medical matters," she said.

"Yes," he said, "he's the medical director."

"Is he also responsible for the nonmedical part of running the hospital ship?" Nancy asked. "Like ordering supplies, meeting federal regulations, and going through customs?"

"Not exactly," Clayton replied. "In most hospitals, such matters are handled by business administrators, not medical professionals."

"Who has those responsibilities for the *Heartliner?*" Nancy watched Clayton intently, but his expression remained charming and courteous.

"The business management of the *Heartliner* will be different for the upcoming trip to the Far East," he answered. "We will release more information when the changes take effect."

Clayton turned his attention to a reporter from the River Heights *Morning Record.* Nancy chewed on her pen, feeling certain Clayton was dodging her question. But why?

The press tour soon broke up, and Nancy walked down the gangway and over to the Pizza Palace. She ordered a medium cheese pizza and waited for Bess and George at a window table. The pizza was soon brought to the table, and the tempting smell of tomatoes and garlic filled her nose. Glancing at her watch, she decided to go ahead and take a piece.

Ten minutes later, the two cousins came charging in the door. "Learn anything interesting?" Nancy asked eagerly, laying down her pizza slice.

George flopped down in a chair and grabbed a slice for herself. "Nothing astonishing," she said. "The *Heartliner* carries big shipments of medicine, medical equipment, books, and magazines down to the areas where they dock. But it's all left there when they leave. They also take toys for the children."

"Isn't that wonderful?" Bess sighed. George offered her some pizza, but she shook her head.

"Bess, stop this," George said. "You have to eat something. If you don't want pizza, order a salad."

"I don't want a salad," Bess said. "I'm going to lose this weight. And if I can't have the pizza, I'd rather have nothing." She slurped her diet soda loudly.

Nancy quietly resolved to talk with Bess about her diet tomorrow, when they were sharing duties for the student field trip. "What else did the nurses say?" she asked.

33

"Well, for one thing, the doctors, nurses, and the staff don't spend all their time on the ship when they're in port," George went on. "Sometimes they set up a tent on shore nearby, where they do simple examinations. Only the really serious cases or those who need surgery are taken aboard the *Heartliner*."

Bess continued. "They also send teams of doctors, nurses, and technicians into the villages. Staff members might stay in a village for days or weeks. They get back on board at a later port, or fly back to the States if the *Heartliner* has already left for home."

"Did you ask them what it's like to work for Sara Lawson?" Nancy asked.

"Actually, they think she's a wonderful nurse and really loves the *Heartliner*," George said. "But they admit she can be impossible to work for. Nurse Wells once drove one of the jeeps into the garage hold forward, instead of backing it in the way they're supposed to, and Lawson grounded her."

"Grounded her?" Nancy asked.

George nodded. "She wouldn't let her go to a fiesta that a village put on in their honor."

"That seems mean," Bess said.

"All the nurses thought so," George agreed.

Next Nancy told her friends about her conversation with Alexander Clayton. "I wonder why he wouldn't give you a straight answer to your question?" Bess remarked.

Nancy chewed her pizza thoughtfully. "I don't know. Maybe he's protecting someone."

"Like Dr. Diaz?" George asked.

Nancy nodded reluctantly. "At any rate, I'd like to find out what that stranger suspects."

"Are you going to tell Maria about the note he gave her dad?" Bess asked.

"Not now," Nancy said with a sigh. "It would only alarm her, and she's worried enough. Let's wait until we know more about this stranger. I'll ask Dr. Diaz himself about him if I have to."

The next morning on the *Heartliner,* Nancy and Bess reported for duty at the eye clinic. Nurse Wells quickly briefed them on the routine. Then galloping footsteps echoed down the companionway, and a swarm of first-graders burst into the clinic. Eyes wide, they stared around at the eye charts and the complicated ophthalmoscopes, which doctors used to look into patients' eyes.

The demonstrations were fun for all. Bess and Nancy helped test each child's vision with eye charts. The nurse wrote a few notes for some children to take home to their parents, recommending follow-up tests. After thirty minutes, the first-graders were herded off to visit another part of the ship. There was a ten-minute break, and then the next group came tumbling in.

The third group came in at eleven o'clock. As Nancy turned to roll down the large eye chart at the front of the room, she was startled to see a tall lanky woman in jeans and a gray sweatshirt walk quickly past the door. Nancy recognized that unmistakable dark red hair—it was Sara Lawson!

"Here, grab the chart," Nancy whispered, holding it out to Bess. "I'll be right back."

Nancy ran out the door. Down the companionway, she saw the woman go into the library. Nancy followed her. As she walked through the doorway, Nurse Lawson sprang out at her. "What do you want?" she demanded.

Introducing herself, Nancy launched into her story about writing a first-person account of working on the ship. The nurse abruptly cut her off. "I saw you at the meeting at the Diaz house," Lawson said. "I'm sure you heard what happened. I'm no longer on the *Heartliner* staff."

"Then what are you doing aboard?" Nancy asked. She could tell she'd struck a nerve. The same angry look came over the nurse's face that she had seen the day before.

"I gave five years of my life to the *Heartliner*," Lawson said, voice trembling. "I won't allow the goals of this ship to be changed!" Shoving Nancy aside, she strode out the door.

Calling out her name, Nancy followed the nurse down two flights of stairs. But as she reached the lower levels of the ship, the red-haired woman seemed to have disappeared. Nancy knew there were lots of places that the nurse could hide aboard ship. Remembering her duty as a hostess, Nancy gave up the chase.

But as she climbed back up the stairs, Nancy mulled over Lawson's bitter words. What did she mean about the ship's goals being changed? Was it something to do with the trip to the Far East?

Bess flashed Nancy a look of relief when she walked back into the eye clinic. The kids waiting to look through the ophthalmoscope were becoming rowdy, and Nancy was soon absorbed in helping to keep order. Before she knew it, it was time to herd the children into the dining salon for lunch.

Each volunteer was asked to sit at a different table of students. A special meal of Latin American foods was being served by the River Heights Cooking Society. Nancy looked up to see one of the members, her family housekeeper, Hannah Gruen, across the room. She smiled and waved.

"Pee-yew!" shouted the boy sitting next to Nancy. "What's that stink?"

Nancy wrinkled her nose and sniffed. The boy was right—a disgusting odor was wafting through the room. It smelled like a thousand rotten eggs.

Looking around the room, Nancy saw kids and adults holding their noses, covering their mouths, and groaning. Nancy's eyes began to water, and her stomach heaved. At the next table, one of the cooking society ladies fainted, dropping a tray of coconut milk shakes all over the floor.

Just then a man at the next table yelled, "Hurry and get out! That's hydrogen sulfide—and it's poison!"

5

A Smelly Clue

Nancy fought to stay calm. Rising to her feet, she called out to the children at her table. "Let's line up and leave the room in an orderly fashion. There's no need to panic."

She grabbed a pile of paper napkins and passed them out to her charges, showing them how to cover their mouths and noses. Then she led the line of children out of the dining salon and up a short flight of stairs to the outer deck.

A nurse on the deck took charge of the children, and Nancy ran back down to the dining salon. All around her, people were coughing and stumbling around in alarm. "Line up and walk this way," she shouted above the din. Slowly, people began to file out of the room.

Behind her napkin mask, Nancy felt a dreadful burning at the back of her throat. She saw the whole scene through tears from her stinging eyes.

She spotted Hannah Gruen kneeling beside her friend, the woman who had fainted. She and Hannah helped the woman into a wheelchair, and Hannah pushed the chair into the companionway toward the elevator.

At last the room was nearly cleared. Nancy wanted to stay and search for the source of the smell, but she didn't dare—she was beginning to feel sick. She left the dining salon with the last group of volunteers and children.

On deck, her lungs gratefully gulped in the cool fresh air, and her head cleared. She joined the end of the crowd moving down the gangway to shore. She could pick out Bess's blond hair and George's dark curls up ahead.

Then she saw a dark blond head bobbing through the crowd. Pushing along the railing was the stranger who had threatened Dr. Diaz!

Stuck in the slow-moving crowd, Nancy couldn't even move. By the time she reached the dock, he had eluded her once again.

Dozens of people were lying on the riverbank grass. An emergency medical services team had arrived from nearby Riverside Hospital, and doctors, nurses, and emergency technicians were walking from student to student. Most already seemed to be recovering from the fumes. A few were being taken to the hospital for observation.

Nancy caught up to Bess and George on the riverbank. "I saw him again," she announced, "the blond stranger, rushing down the gangway."

"Maybe he was responsible for the gas cloud," Bess said breathlessly.

"Maybe, maybe not. I also saw Sara Lawson on board before the gas was released." Nancy went on to tell them about her confrontation with the red-haired nurse in the library. "Did either of you see her leave the ship?" she asked.

Bess and George shook their heads. "Maybe she's still in the poison air!" Bess cried.

"Well, not for long," George said. "Here come the police."

Turning, Nancy spotted Detective Brody stepping out of an unmarked car on Front Street. She'd worked with him on several cases before. Pushing through the crowd, she went to talk to him.

"You always seem to be on hand when there's trouble, Nancy," Brody greeted her with a smile. "So what do you know about this incident?"

Quickly Nancy told him about the mysterious stranger with the mustache. She also told him about Sara Lawson, and she offered to show him the library, where she'd last seen Lawson.

Brody raised his eyebrows. "We can't go on board yet," he said. "The chemical investigation squad has to analyze what's in the air before anybody can return to the ship." He pointed to a small squad of people on the bank, dressed in bright yellow jumpsuits with boots, gloves, and hoods with masks. They were strapping on oxygen tanks before boarding the ship. Another

41

officer was blocking off the gangway with yellow tapes that read Do Not Enter—Police Investigation in Progress.

"Hang around for a little while until they're done," Brody suggested to Nancy. "I could use your help investigating the crime scene."

Nancy agreed to meet the detective in half an hour. While he went off to interview other witnesses, she rejoined her friends.

The riverbank was rapidly clearing now. A line of yellow schoolbuses near the dock was filling up with schoolchildren to take them home.

In the press tent that had been set up for yesterday's events, Dr. Diaz summoned all the volunteers. Nancy noticed how distraught he looked. With a minimum of words, he dismissed the volunteers for the day. "We'll call you all tonight to tell you whether we will be conducting field trips tomorrow," he said wearily.

As the volunteers dispersed, Nancy turned to Pepe, who was talking to Maria, Bess, and George. "I need more of a look at the *Heartliner* than we've had so far," she said thoughtfully. "Pepe, could you give Bess, George, and me a grand tour?"

"Show you around my former home?" Pepe said. "*Sí*, I would enjoy that very much."

"Maria, could you come, too?" Nancy asked. "I'm sure you've been aboard many times."

"Sure," Maria answered. "How about tomorrow night, about seven-thirty? I'm going with

Mom this evening to my cousin's baby shower, and right now I'm going to the hospital—I need to hitch a ride home with Dad."

Arrangements were quickly made, and Maria walked off to the hospital. George and Bess offered to give Pepe a ride home. Nancy went back to the gangway to meet Detective Brody.

The chemical investigation squad was trooping down the gangway as she arrived there. "The air's no longer hazardous," the squad chief was saying to Detective Brody. "You can go on up."

"Thanks," Brody said. He crooked a finger at Nancy, held up the yellow tape for her to duck underneath, and walked with her up the gangway.

First they went to the dining salon, where they met a second policeman, Officer Horton. He showed them a detailed blueprint of the *Heartliner*.

"The gas seemed to come from the galley," Nancy told them, pointing toward the ship's kitchen. The policemen followed her into the long, narrow room.

"I can still smell the stuff," Officer Horton said, grimacing. Portable fans were whirring on the countertops, still clearing the air.

Nancy opened the door to the pantry. The stench was stronger there. "Hey, I think I found something," she said. She pointed to a shelf next to the ventilation duct, where a shallow pan sat.

Wearing gloves, Detective Brody removed the

43

pan and inspected it. A few traces of liquid lay glimmering on the bottom. Brody slid the pan into a plastic evidence bag. "Get this to the lab right away," he said to Officer Horton, who carried the bag out of the galley at arm's length.

Detective Brody and Nancy went on to inspect the library. In the companionway, they met Nurse Wells, who was helping the investigators find their way around the ship. "Do you have a diagram of the ship?" Nancy asked the nurse.

"No," Nurse Wells answered. "But there are several copies in the closet in the library."

Entering the library, Nancy and the detective fought off the foul-smelling air. Nancy stepped over and opened one of the porthole windows. She and Brody searched the room while she repeated her account of her meeting with Nurse Lawson.

Spotting a door in the back corner of the room, between two tall bookcases, Nancy said, "There's the closet—let me look for those diagrams."

She opened the door to the small supply closet. Looks as if someone left here in a hurry, she thought to herself. Papers and office supplies were shoved against the back wall and littered over the floor.

Finally she found the copies of the ship's diagrams in a jumbled pile on the floor. As she picked them up, her eyes widened.

There on the floor lay a small empty glass vial labeled ammonium sulfide.

She picked up the bottle carefully, using a tissue to shield her hand. Even with the stopper in, the smell was unmistakable—rotten eggs!

"Detective?" she called out. "I think this may be a useful clue. I'll bet you'll find that the liquid in that pan is ammonium sulfide from this vial."

Running over to the closet, Brody slipped on his gloves and took the vial. "Good work, Nancy!" he exclaimed. "Let me run up on deck and try to catch Horton before he leaves for the lab. Then you can show me where you found it."

As he hurried out of the library, Nancy glanced over the closet. Was it just coincidence that the vial had been found in the room where she'd seen Nurse Lawson earlier?

Taking a copy of the ship's diagram, Nancy studied it intently. Then suddenly she heard footsteps pounding down the companionway toward the elevator.

Senses alert, Nancy peeked out of the library toward the sound. The elevator door had just swooshed shut.

That's funny, thought Nancy. No one was supposed to be on the ship except the police. And why would a police officer be running like that? Acting on impulse, she ran to the stairwell and raced the elevator to the lower decks.

She could hear the elevator cables grinding, and she kept running down the steps until she heard them stop. She was at the bottom of the stairway—the lowest deck.

45

Her instincts told her to stay hidden and not surprise the person. She stayed in the stairwell until she heard the footsteps leave the elevator, running loud and fast.

She stepped into the companionway. In the distance she heard a door slam. She walked quickly down the hall, but there was no sign of activity. She turned the handles to all the doors in that hall, but all were locked.

Frustrated, Nancy returned to the elevator and rode it up to the main deck, looking for Detective Brody. She spotted him on shore, talking to someone in his squad car. She walked back down the gangway and waited for him, meanwhile glancing over the diagram in her hand.

Just then her attention was caught by a flurry of activity. A clutch of reporters had gathered on the riverbank, and they'd just caught sight of Alexander Clayton walking calmly down the gangway. He paused at the foot of the ramp to speak to the press.

"We'll know a lot more after the initial investigation is completed," she heard Clayton saying. "It was terrible, but it could have been much worse, of course. All those dear schoolchildren . . ."

Clayton shook his head sadly. "I was in Mapleton—about an hour from here—attending a board of directors meeting for Citizens Power and Light when I got word. Naturally, I came immediately."

"What do you think caused the odor?" demanded one of the reporters.

Clayton smiled. "I'm sure the final analysis will show that this was an accident," he said. "That doesn't excuse whoever might be responsible, of course. I'm posting a reward of five thousand dollars for any information about the incident."

Spotting Detective Brody, he waved away the reporters and strode over to the police officer. Nancy sidled over to join them.

"Hello, Detective Brody," Clayton said. "I trust you're supervising this investigation personally." Turning to see Nancy, he added, "And, Ms. Drew, how nice to see you again. Were you aboard during the accident?"

"Yes. It was frightening," she said.

"Well, this shall make for some interesting paragraphs in your first-person account of the week," he said. "If you think of any information that will help the authorities, please let them know—the five thousand dollars could be yours."

"If there's anything to be found, Nancy will find it," Detective Brody said. "She's quite an amateur detective."

"Is that so?" Clayton said politely, nodding his head. The sun glinted off his gold cuff link as he shook Detective Brody's hand and left.

Nancy and Detective Brody spent twenty more minutes on board the ship but found no new evidence. Promising to call her if anything else

47

turned up, the detective got in his car and drove away. Nancy walked to her car, lost in thought.

Looking up, she was surprised to see Maria Diaz on the sidewalk, looking anxiously around.

"Have you seen my dad?" she asked Nancy. "No one knows where he is. After the police came, he told me he was going back to the hospital, but his nurse says he never arrived."

Nancy wondered if Maria was right to be worried. Had the blond stranger caught up with her father?

"I'll drive you home," Nancy offered. "Maybe he's there."

Maria sat glumly beside Nancy in the car. She didn't say much as Nancy drove to the Diazes' neighborhood. Then, as Nancy made the turn onto their street, Maria burst out, "Nancy, you *have* to find out what's going on! Dad was already upset about something. Now this nasty incident with that awful smell—what if any of those children had been hurt?"

"Luckily, it seems no one *was* badly affected," Nancy said to soothe her friend.

Suddenly Maria clutched at the dashboard. "Watch out!" she yelled, pointing ahead.

A black car swerved out of the Diaz drive right in front of them. Nancy stomped on the brakes, narrowly missing the car.

As it surged past, Nancy had just an instant to see the driver, but that's all she needed. It was the blond stranger again!

"Do you recognize that person?" Nancy asked Maria levelly.

"I have no idea who it was," Maria replied in a frightened voice. "What was he doing at our house? Oh, hurry, Nancy—hurry!"

Nancy skidded to a stop in front of the Diaz home. Her heart dropped when she saw the front door slightly ajar. She and Maria ran into the house, while Maria called out, "Dad! Mom! Where is everyone!"

Nancy spotted a note on the foyer table. " 'Maria,' " Nancy read aloud. "Your father's working. Come to the club and help with the shower. Love, Mother.' "

Maria went dashing off into her father's study, Nancy following right behind. But before Nancy could reach the room, she heard Maria let out a piercing scream!

6

Going Down, Down, Down

Nancy burst into the study and ran to Maria's side. Maria stood next to her father's desk, her hands over her mouth. Dr. Diaz lay on the floor between the wall and the desk.

"Dr. Diaz! Dr. Diaz!" Nancy called to him.

His hair was mussed, and one of the pockets of his lab coat was torn. His head lolled on a messy pillow of file folders and forms. With a glance, Nancy noticed that the papers were the *Heartliner* files that she and Maria had studied.

"Dr. Diaz! Can you hear me?" Nancy said, gently. She checked his pulse. It was normal, and his breathing was natural.

Then Dr. Diaz moaned. He reached for the back of his head and then for his rib cage. Eyes fluttering open, he struggled to sit up.

"Maria, don't worry," he murmured. "I'm

50

okay." He was obviously sore as he rose to his feet, assisted by Nancy. She helped him over to a large dark green leather chair.

"I'll call for help," Nancy offered.

"No!" Dr. Diaz said. "That's not necessary. I'm fine—it was just a little fall."

"Dad, please!" Maria said. "Let me call Dr. Arnstein. He can look you over."

"No, Maria," he said firmly. "I'm a doctor, and I know when I need help and when I don't."

"What happened to you, Dr. Diaz?" Nancy asked. The picture of the mysterious stranger driving away down the street flashed through her mind. "You say you fell?"

"Yes," he answered. "I was on the stool, getting a book from that top shelf. I lost my balance and fell backward. I must have hit my head on the desk and knocked myself out."

Nancy glanced over toward the desk. The small, one-step stool was keeled over on its side.

Dr. Diaz stood up shakily and moved to escort them to the door. "I appreciate your concern, but I feel just fine." Wincing, he gave the girls a broad but false-looking smile.

Before they could say more, Nancy and Maria were in the hall. Dr. Diaz closed his study door behind them, and Nancy heard an extra click. He had locked the door!

Nancy and Maria walked out slowly to the driveway. "Nancy, whatever happened to Dad tonight—do you think that strange man had something to do with it?" Maria asked in a small, frightened voice once they were outside.

"I don't know," Nancy said grimly, "but I'm going to find out."

They drove off in their separate cars, Maria to the shower and Nancy to her own home. As she drove, Nancy thought about her next step. She knew she had to find out who that blond man was.

When she walked in the back door of her house, her father, Carson Drew, was sitting in the kitchen with Hannah. "You just got a phone call from Nurse Wells," Mr. Drew reported. "She said the ship has been okayed for activity tomorrow. You're to report at eight A.M."

Hannah frowned. "What if that horrible-smelling poison is still around?"

"The chemical investigators checked it out thoroughly," Nancy said. "But just to be sure—"

She trotted upstairs and got out her high school chemistry textbook. Sitting at the kitchen table, she pored over it while she filled in her father and Hannah on the day's events.

"Look here," she finally located the right passage in the book. "It says that hydrogen sulfide is a poison, but ammonium sulfide isn't. It smells just as bad, though, and it can make you sick to your stomach."

"You're telling me!" Hannah agreed. "Maybe it was set off by accident during a field trip."

"No," Nancy answered. "Somebody would have told the police if that were true. I'm afraid it was someone trying to sabotage the ship's activities. Now I just have to find out who—and why."

At eight o'clock the next morning, Tuesday, the *Heartliner* hostesses and hosts met on the dock with the nurses. Nancy and Pepe were assigned to the admissions area, and Bess, George, and Maria were working in the ENT clinic—*ENT* meaning ear, nose, and throat.

"I like admissions," Pepe said to Nancy as they entered the area. "I worked in admissions in our last port, a small village in Costa Rica." His usual grin faded as he remembered. "The people who live there don't get enough food, and what they do get is lacking in vitamins A, B, and C, calcium and iron. It's a very sad place."

"You really enjoy working in medicine," Nancy commented, pulling on a lab coat. "And Dr. Diaz—do you think he's a good doctor?" she added, hoping Pepe might offer her a clue.

"A good doctor and a good man," Pepe said. "It is because of him that I am alive today. And it is because of him that I come to your beautiful country and go to medical school."

The serious moment was broken with a jolt as thirty ten-year-old students burst into the room.

The nurses bustled around, but Pepe ran the show that morning. "The first thing we do when the *Heartliner* docks is set up an admissions tent on shore," he told the students. "When the sick people come in, we check their blood pressure and listen to their pulses and heartbeats."

While he talked, Nancy and the nurse took the stethoscope and showed the students how to check pulses and listen to one another's heartbeats.

Pepe walked over to a ten-year-old girl with a long braid. "What is your name?" he asked, taking her pulse, his eyes on his watch.

"Melissa," she said. Nancy watched Pepe proceed to charm the little girl out of her shyness. He took a wide, flat wooden stick and said, "Open your mouth and say 'Ah.' This stick is called a tongue depressor. It holds your tongue down while I look at the back of your mouth and throat for redness or swelling."

He smiled at the students, saying, "Doctors and nurses are like detectives. They look in your eyes, listen to your voice, and look at your skin— always checking for clues."

Nancy smiled—it was a good comparison. Then Nurse Chang whispered to her, "Would you please go to the medical supply hold and get us some more tongue depressors? It's the room directly under the dining salon."

Nancy walked down the companionway to the stairs and then went down one deck. The door to the supply hold was directly below the door to the dining salon. But when Nancy went inside, she noticed something different about it immediately. The far wall of the dining salon had windows, Nancy remembered—it was in the outer wall of the ship. But the supply hold had no windows.

Just to be sure, she went back up to check the dining salon. She paced off the lengths of its walls, then went back downstairs and paced off the lengths of the supply hold's walls. The supply hold wasn't deep enough to reach the outside of the ship, Nancy realized. There must be another room behind this one, she thought, but there's no door to it from in here.

She stepped back out in the companionway and looked for another door there. Most of the doors were locked. Frowning, she made a mental note to check out those rooms when Pepe gave her, Bess, George, and Maria their private tour that evening.

At seven-thirty sharp Nancy parked her car on Front Street. She, Bess, and George walked the short distance to the gangway.

Pepe and Maria were up on deck waiting for them. "Nancy, Bess, George," Pepe said, as the girls walked up the gangway. "This is Manuel Valencia, the *Heartliner*'s night watchman. He guards the ship while the crew is on leave." Pepe gestured toward a stocky, gray-haired man dressed in navy blue coveralls. Turning to him, Pepe said, "You do not need to escort us tonight, Manuel. I have my own keys." He pulled an impressive ring of keys from his jeans pocket.

"You have become a real somebody now, Pepe," Manuel said with a low whistle. "You have your own keys." Waving to the girls, Manuel sat back down and picked up his magazine.

Nancy and her friends followed Pepe into the companionway. "Did we pull it off?" Pepe asked.

"You were great, Pepe," Maria said. She turned to Nancy and explained, "I borrowed Dad's keys and had them copied at the mall."

"How is your dad, Maria?" George asked. "Nancy told us he fell last night."

"He's fine—at least physically," Maria sighed. "But he was really jumpy today, and he seems so angry all the time now. He—he's just not acting like my dad." Her voice trembled.

"Perhaps we can find out something tonight that will help explain why your father's so upset," Nancy said gently. "The two sets of records for the last cruise declared two different weights. Maybe we can find evidence that something was hidden on the ship when it returned to the States."

"You mean something was smuggled aboard the *Heartliner?*" Maria looked at Nancy in disbelief.

"Could be," Nancy said. "At the meeting on

56

Saturday, I heard Sara Lawson say that several weird things happened during the last cruise. Do you know what she was talking about, Pepe?"

"There *was* one thing I thought was strange," Pepe recalled. "The entire sailing crew—thirty-one men—left at Buenos Aires, and a whole new crew reported that evening."

"Did anyone say why?" Nancy asked.

"No," Pepe answered. "No one ever knew whether the first crew was fired or just quit."

Pepe led them down to the lower decks. The copied keys worked well, opening all the doors. Nancy and her friends looked through a medicine hold, a food storage hold, staff sleeping quarters, a radio room, rest rooms, and an office.

"This is the floor I'm most interested in," Nancy said when they reached the lowest deck. First they took a look inside the medical supply hold Nancy had been in that afternoon. Then they checked the next two doors on that side of the companionway, finding a laundry room and a boiler room. They were all the same depth— none of them reached the outer wall of the ship.

Nancy stopped to spread out her copy of the ship's diagram on a wall. "See?" she showed her friends. "Behind these rooms is this long L-shaped room, which stretches along the outer wall of the ship. This last door on this side should lead to it—it's labeled as the garage hold."

"That *does* go all the way to the outside of the

ship," Pepe stated. "You can drive a jeep up a ramp into it, right from the dock. The doctors and nurses need the jeeps to make trips into the countryside to visit the sick."

Inside, the garage hold looked like a filling station. Tools, tires, and other auto supplies were stacked in the corners. Two dented, dusty jeeps were parked in the middle of the room. A pair of large doors on the far wall allowed the jeeps to be driven in and out.

Picking her way around the equipment, Nancy walked around a corner where the hold turned to make an L. But it was a very short L, ending in a solid wall with a small door. "This part of the room should run the length of the ship," Nancy said, studying the diagram again.

She opened the door to find a closet full of mechanics' coveralls, boots, and gloves.

Nancy frowned and stepped back, looking around the room. "Don't you notice some-thing strange about this wall?" she asked. "It's not exactly the same color as the other three walls."

"It *is* a lighter shade than the rest," Maria agreed, following Nancy's gaze.

"Maybe it's not a lighter shade," Nancy said. "Maybe it's just freshly painted." Stepping back into the little closet, she pushed the mechanics' jumpsuits aside to reveal the back wall. Boards had been nailed neatly across it, covering the

entire surface. "Apparently, the long room was walled off," Nancy said thoughtfully. "I wonder how recently, and why."

George leaned over and tugged at one of the boards, but it was nailed securely.

"Let's see what's across the companionway from this hold," Nancy suggested. "From the diagram, it looks like it's the same long L shape. But there's no label for it on the diagram."

Pepe opened the door across the companion-way and switched on the light. They were in a mirror image of the room they had just left—an L-shaped room. The short part of the L clearly extended to the outside of the ship, because there were boarded-up portholes on the far wall. Otherwise, the room was empty.

Nancy walked around the corner into the long part of the L. It seemed to run the entire length of the ship, and it was crammed with pieces of heavy machinery.

"What on earth . . . ?" George gasped softly, coming up behind her.

"It looks like a factory," Nancy said. "One that's been hit by a tornado."

Nancy walked a few yards into the storage area, but the machinery was crammed in so tight she couldn't go any farther. There were parts stacked everywhere: motors and platforms, cables, winches, pumps, and what looked like enormous copper mixing bowls and huge stirring paddles.

At the far end stood what looked like a conveyor belt.

"Maybe this is stuff left over from the old navy days," George suggested.

"I don't know," Nancy answered doubtfully.

"I don't remember anyone ever talking about this room," Pepe said. "It's always been locked."

"Do you think this is what makes the weight difference on the two sets of records, Nancy?" Maria asked.

"If it is, I don't know why it was smuggled in," Nancy murmured.

The group stayed a while longer but could turn up no clues. Nancy finally suggested they head home.

"I'm taking the elevator." Bess sighed, punching the button on the wall. "I've been on my feet all day." The others joined her, crowding through the doors into the small space.

Inside, George pushed the button, and the elevator wheezed as it began its ascent.

Then, as they neared the main deck, the elevator car lurched. "What's happening!" Bess shrieked.

The elevator was starting to fall back down!

The force of the fall slammed Nancy against the back wall. She saw Maria and Pepe tumble into the corner by the control panels. Bess sat down with a rude thump, while George threw out

her arms for balance, riding the elevator like a surfboard.

Nancy desperately jabbed at the control buttons, one after the other, but none of them made any difference.

Suddenly the light went out and the elevator stopped!

7

The Missing Link

"Is everyone all right?" Nancy asked in a hushed voice. "Bess? Maria? George?"

"I'm okay," George said.

"Well, I'm not all right," Bess said in a grumpy voice. "I'm scared. What's going on?"

Maria's small voice came from the corner of the elevator cab. "I banged into the wall pretty hard," she said, "but I'll live."

Nancy reached into her purse for a small flashlight. "Pepe, let me have the keys," Nancy ordered. "George, you hold the flashlight beam on the elevator panel." She quickly found a small phone receiver attached to the wall. But when she tried to call for help on it, the line was dead.

Meanwhile Bess pushed the elevator emergency button again and again. There was no sound—no response at all.

62

Nancy trained the flashlight on the big ring of keys. "Here's one marked Elevator," she announced. "Now, if we can just find the lock." George angled the tiny beam of light around, and all five of them hunted for the lock.

Nancy finally saw it at the top of one of the doors. She fitted in the key. It worked!

The doors eased open a crack, and George and Pepe pried them all the way open. The elevator had stopped about two feet down from the third deck, but everyone was able to scramble up onto the companionway floor. Glancing around, Nancy saw that all the ship's electricity was off, not just the elevators.

Relying on his knowledge of the ship, Pepe led them down the dark hall toward the stairs, using Nancy's penlight as a tiny beacon. They held hands in a long single file: Pepe first, then Nancy, Maria, Bess, and George. Nancy could feel Pepe's strong, reassuring touch in front of her, and Maria's trembling, frightened hand behind.

At last they reached the main deck and stepped out into the clear May night. The stars blinked overhead, and the lights of River Heights shimmered beyond the riverbank. Pepe and Nancy ran to Manuel, who lay snoring on a long deck chair, a magazine spread out on his large belly.

"Manuel, wake up," Pepe yelled. "There's something wrong with the electricity!"

"What do you mean?" Manuel asked, shaking

63

his head groggily. He pointed to the light coming from the companionway just off the deck. "The lights are working."

Nancy turned, surprised, to see the light. Curious, she trotted back inside to check out the elevator.

When she pushed the button, the doors slid open immediately on the main deck level, aligned perfectly with the floor. She picked up the phone and heard a dial tone. She pushed the emergency button and heard the usual urgent buzz.

Nancy silently joined her friends back by the watchman's chair. Calling good night to Manuel, they filed quietly down the gangway.

When they reached their cars, Nancy turned to Maria. "I'd like to borrow the keys," she said, "to do some more exploring another time."

Maria handed her the key ring. "Keep them as long as you like."

They all exchanged subdued goodbyes. Pepe and Maria climbed into their car, and Bess and George joined Nancy in her Mustang.

"Was it just a temporary power outage?" George asked Nancy as she started the engine.

"I know that's what Pepe thinks," Nancy said. "And it's possible. But it could be that we weren't alone on that ship tonight."

No one spoke the rest of the way home.

* * *

The next morning was a cool, rainy Wednesday. Nancy was driving Bess and George to the *Heartliner*. "You two are invited over for dinner tonight," Nancy said as she parked her Mustang. "We can talk over this case. I can tell you what happens at today's press conference, when Detective Brody releases the results of the lab analysis of the gas we smelled on Monday."

On board the ship, Bess checked the board to learn their assignments for the day. "George, you're doing X ray today, Pepe's in physiotherapy, and Maria's in admissions," she said. "Nancy, you and I are in one of the patient wards."

They all went off to their morning duty. Nancy and Bess were working with Nurses Wells and Chang, showing the students how patients were cared for in the wards. They demonstrated how patients were moved from a stretcher onto a bed, and how sheets could be changed under them by rolling the patients back and forth.

The kids seemed fascinated by the beds. Each bunk hung from the ceiling by heavy chains so that patients would not feel the normal lurching of the ship. The room filled with the sound of creaking metal as students climbed on the beds to see what they felt like.

During her lunch break, Nancy went ashore, running through the soft spring rain to the press tent. She arrived just as Dr. Diaz began.

"We're glad to announce that the substance

released in the dining salon on Monday was not the poison hydrogen sulfide," he stated. "It was ammonium sulfide, a gas that smells nauseating but isn't toxic."

"We still haven't determined what caused the gas to be released," Detective Brody added, "but our investigation continues. It appears it was an accident, but we haven't ruled out the possibility that it was a prank or vandalism."

Dr. Diaz asked for questions from the small group of reporters. A voice spoke up behind Nancy. "Dr. Diaz, I'm David Conner of the Washington *Investigative Journal.* Do you think this incident is connected to the mass firing of the sailing crew in Buenos Aires during the ship's last Latin American tour?"

A surprised murmur rose from the reporters. Nancy turned to look toward the voice and started with shock. It was the mysterious blond man with the droopy mustache!

Dr. Diaz answered curtly. "Of course not. All organizations have occasional problems with personnel. Now, if you'll excuse me, I have patients to see." He strode out of the tent, leaving Detective Brody with the reporters.

Nancy hurried after Maria's father, determined to get some answers. "Dr. Diaz, wait a minute, please."

The doctor turned, waving for Nancy to join him under his black umbrella. "What is it, Nancy? I'm due at the hospital," he said uneasily.

"That man back there—David Conner. Do you know him?" she asked intently.

"Why do you ask?" Dr. Diaz shifted his weight from foot to foot.

"I've seen him near you three times before, and each time was unpleasant," she said. Briefly she told him about Conner peeking in the Diaz kitchen Saturday night and driving away from the Diaz home Monday night. "I'm sure he was running down the gangway after the ammonium sulfide was released," she concluded, "and I also saw him bump into you behind the press tent Sunday." She decided not to mention that she'd found the note.

"I have met Mr. Conner before," Dr. Diaz admitted. "What are you implying?"

"Nothing," Nancy said. "I just wondered if he was threatening you in any way." Nancy saw Dr. Diaz frown and sensed she had gone too far.

"What do you mean, threatening?" Dr. Diaz glared at her. "You must watch yourself, young lady. That's the kind of speculation that leads to vicious rumors!" He stormed off, leaving Nancy standing alone in the rain.

She ran back to the press tent and found Conner getting coffee. "Mr. Conner, I'd like to talk to you," she said breathlessly.

"Oh, really? And who are you?" he asked.

He seemed to be pretending that he'd never seen her before, so she decided to confront him directly. "My name is Nancy Drew. Just why are you in River Heights? And what are you doing peeking in people's windows?''

He grabbed her arm and pulled her away from the others. "Quiet," he snarled. "I don't want anyone to know why I'm here. This is my story."

"Field trips aboard a floating hospital?" Nancy looked skeptical. "That's not investigative journalism material. But how about assault on the ship's chief of staff? I saw you drive away from the Diaz house Monday night—driving as if you were leaving the scene of a crime."

"I don't know what you mean," Conner muttered, shifting his eyes away from her gaze.

"Detective Brody?" Nancy called over to the police officer. "Could you come here a minute?"

"Okay, okay, I was there that night," Conner muttered. "I'll tell you about it—privately."

Nancy waved to Detective Brody. "Just wanted to say goodbye!" she called out, and he returned her wave as he left the tent. She turned back to David Conner.

Glancing nervously around, he began his story. "I was going to interview Dr. Diaz at his home that night—I'd made an appointment. But when I got there, the front door was ajar. That seemed odd, so I walked in. I found him in his study, lying on the floor, unconscious."

"What time was that?" Nancy asked.

"About six o'clock," Conner answered. "I didn't want to be there when the family came home—my meeting was with him and only him

—so I thought I'd stop at a pay phone and call for help anonymously. When I saw you and his daughter driving up, I knew you'd find him and get help, so I just left. That's it—end of story."

"And what about Monday afternoon?" she asked. "What were you doing on the ship when the gas was released?"

"Stop trying to play detective," Conner said sarcastically. "You're going to get in deeper than you should. This is a big story, bigger than your flaky little River Heights problems."

Conner crunched his plastic coffee cup, threw it away, and stalked out of the tent. Nancy flushed with anger as she watched him go. "We'll just see about that," she muttered, and she headed back up the gangway onto the ship.

She popped her head into the patient ward, promising Bess that she'd be back as soon as she got dried off. Then she headed to the library, glad to see that there was no one there. Closing the door, she went to the desk and picked up the phone there.

The information operator gave her the number of the Washington *Investigative Journal*. Charging the call to her home phone, she spoke to the editor, asking for David Conner's credentials.

"Yes, we do have a David Conner on our staff," the editor admitted. "But I can't tell you where he is or what he's working on."

"If I describe him, can you tell me if it's the same guy?" Nancy asked.

"No, I can't. And since our reporters often work undercover, he may be in disguise anyway," the editor replied, hanging up abruptly.

As Nancy ran a comb through her wet hair, she wondered if Conner's droopy light brown mustache was possibly part of a disguise. Pondering the case, she headed back toward the patient wardroom.

When she entered, she saw several kids climbing in and out of the patient beds. A nine-year-old girl was climbing into one of the lower bunks. Other students were clamoring for Hostess Bess to climb into the upper bunk.

With a grin, Bess climbed the short ladder and hoisted one leg over the edge of the bed. As she leaned in to bring her other leg up, Nancy's heart leapt into her throat.

The chains holding the double-decker bunks were quivering and about to break in two!

"Bess, no!" Nancy yelled.

The lower bunk hit the floor with a loud thunk. Everyone watched in terror as the heavy metal bed carrying Bess headed straight down toward the girl in the lower bunk!

8

Girl Overboard!

Without pausing, Nancy bounded over the floor to the fallen bed and pulled the girl out of it.

Gripping the edges of the bed and screaming, Bess rode the top bunk down. It landed on top of the other bed with a horrible metallic crash. The pillow where the girl had been lying moments before was squished between the two beds.

"You're okay," Nancy soothed the girl, who was trembling and clinging tightly to Nancy. Nancy handed her over to Nurse Wells and ran to her friend.

Bess had been thrown against the wall, jamming her elbow. As Nurse Chang took her arm to move her onto another bed, Bess wailed. "Ooooh, that hurts."

"Lie down, Bess," the nurse said. "We'll send one of the doctors down to look at that arm."

71

"Can you handle the kids?" Nancy asked the nurses. "I'd like to stay with Bess."

Nurse Wells nodded and led the anxious band of nine-year-olds off to the lounge. Nancy knelt beside Bess's bed and chatted to distract her from the pain.

In a few minutes, a young doctor arrived. He was very cute, with thick fair hair, deep hazel eyes, and a dimple when he smiled. "Hi," he said, "I'm Jack Herman. I understand you've been riding a bucking bunk."

Nancy saw Bess perk up immediately as she turned her attention to the young doctor. Seeing that her friend was in good hands, Nancy turned to inspect the site of the accident.

The heavy chains that had held the beds were lying on the floor where they had fallen. Nancy picked one up and examined its thick steel links. At the spot where the link had broken, she noticed, the edges were smooth three quarters of the way through but jagged the rest of the way. A quick inspection showed her that the other three chains were all broken the same way.

Nancy's heart sank. Could the chains have been tampered with? She detached one of the broken links and slipped it into the pocket of her slacks to take to Detective Brody.

"I think we need an X ray of that arm," Dr. Herman told Bess. "Why don't you two come with me? Bess, you'll make a perfect X-ray demonstration for the field trips."

Dr. Herman led Nancy and Bess down the companionway to the radiology lab, where a group of twelve-year-olds was gathered. An X ray soon showed that Bess's arm was sprained, not broken. Dr. Herman led her off to the physiotherapy room to fit her with a plastic splint and a sling. By the end of the day, Bess had been featured on so many field trips, she was the star of the ship.

Nancy and Bess met George in the parking lot at five o'clock. "What a day you two have had," George said, patting Bess on the back.

"Don't forget dinner tonight," Nancy said as George helped Bess into her car. "Bess, do you think you should skip it?"

"Are you kidding?" Bess answered. "Miss one of Hannah Gruen's barbecues? Not on your life."

On her way home, Nancy took a detour to the central police station, where she told Detective Brody about Bess's accident. "Look at this," she said, laying the broken chain link on his desk blotter. "What do you think?"

He looked at it closely under his desk lamp. "What do I think? I think I'm sorry it broke and I'm glad no one was hurt too badly."

"But look," Nancy persisted, pointing. "It's smooth along here and jagged the rest of the way. All four chains were like that."

"What are you saying?" the detective asked.

"Could they have been sawed partway through

73

so that they'd break the rest of the way when someone climbed onto the bed?" Nancy suggested.

"Of course, they could have," Brody admitted, feeling the broken edge with his finger. "But I think it was probably a manufacturing defect."

Nancy shook her head stubbornly. "First there was the 'accidental' release of gas," she pointed out. "Then the 'accidental' breaking of a hanging bunk, plus an 'accidental' temporary loss of electricity." She briefly told him what had happened the night before with the elevator. "It all seems very suspicious to me."

"All right." He sighed, raising his eyebrows. "I'll check out the chain link. And just to be safe, I don't want you sneaking around that ship on your own—no more private tours."

It was a beautiful evening for a cookout. Nancy led Bess and George through the kitchen out to the flagstone terrace of the Drews' patio. The sun had come out earlier that afternoon and dried the redwood furniture. "How's your arm, Bess?" Nancy asked.

"It hurts," Bess said, wincing, "but I'm okay."

The three girls took their usual seats—Nancy in the armchair, George sprawled on the glider, Bess on the lounge. They had been talking only a few moments when Nancy's father, Carson, joined them. A noted criminal lawyer, he had dark hair that was graying at the temples.

"Hi, girls," he said, smiling at Bess and George as he gave Nancy a hug. "Bess, I heard that a hostess had sprained her arm today. Don't tell me it was you." He eyed her splint.

"I'm afraid so," Bess replied with a sigh.

Carson started grilling the chicken while Nancy recounted the day's adventure for him.

Hannah Gruen, who had been the Drews' housekeeper since Nancy's mother died many years earlier, brought out two wonderful salads. One had red potatoes and crunchy snow peas with vinaigrette dressing; the other had cherry tomatoes, yellow plum tomatoes, zucchini, and onion in a sweet-and-sour poppyseed dressing.

They were still talking about the *Heartliner* when they all sat down to eat. Nancy changed the subject when she saw Bess take only a teaspoonful of each of the salads.

"Bess, listen to me," Nancy said, exasperated. "This starvation diet has to stop."

"What's this?" her father added. "You're not eating any of my chicken, Bess?"

"Maybe you can talk some sense into her, Dad," Nancy pleaded.

"Bess, if you want to lose a few pounds, you have to use your head," he said gently. "Everything on this table is healthy if you eat a moderate amount. Now, please, don't let me down. Tell me how I did with the chicken."

Sighing, Bess took a small chicken breast and let Hannah put more of the salads on her plate. "Okay, but you weren't there today, Mr. Drew," Bess said. "I climbed into a bed and the whole thing collapsed. If I were thinner, that bed wouldn't have broken."

"Bess, no! That's not true." Nancy told them about the chain link and her conversation with Detective Brody. Then she recounted her conversations earlier that day with Dr. Diaz and David Conner.

"Do you know the Diazes?" Bess asked Carson. "Maria has been a good friend of mine from the moment they moved here from San Diego. I'd just die if her father was in trouble."

"I've met Armando, of course, because I'm on Riverside Hospital's board of directors," Mr. Drew said. "But I don't really know him that well. He certainly has an excellent reputation."

He passed the chicken. "I know Francesca professionally," he added, "but I don't know her all that well personally. She's a very good attorney."

"Dr. Diaz acts as if he's hiding something, Dad," Nancy said. "If you could have seen how his mood changed this afternoon . . . and I know he isn't being completely truthful about how he got knocked out the other night."

"Let me run a check on the Diazes, Nancy," Mr. Drew said. "I have a friend who's chief of San

Diego's Mercury Hospital. I'll see what I can find out."

"I wish I knew what David Conner is up to, too," Nancy said. "How can we check up on him?"

"I heard one of the journalists say they were sticking around awhile because of the strange things going on on the *Heartliner*," George mentioned. "Most of them are staying at the Riverview Suites."

Nancy perked up. "Why don't we go over there and see if we can find out anything from the other reporters? I'll bet the other members of the press corps keep tabs on one another."

As soon as dinner was over, the girls climbed into Nancy's car and headed for the hotel. The Riverview Suites Hotel was located at the end of a bridge across the Muskoka River, on the opposite bank from the *Heartliner*'s dock.

As Nancy drove over the bridge, she noticed a young man walking in the opposite direction, away from the hotel and toward the ship. He wore a baseball cap, and his head was down, but there was no mistaking the droopy mustache.

"There he goes," Nancy said, pointing out Conner to her friends. She turned the car around and drove back across the river. Conner was walking along the bank toward the *Heartliner* as they drove up behind him.

Keeping a discreet distance, Nancy parked on

Front Street. The girls sprinted over to the ship in time to see Conner on the upper deck, just disappearing around a corner.

"Where's Manuel?" George whispered as they went up the gangway. His chair stood empty.

"I don't know," Nancy whispered back. "At least we won't have to explain to him what we're doing here."

"Maybe Conner knocked him out," Bess said, her voice shaky. "Nancy, I don't like this. We should go home."

"We won't stay long," Nancy assured her. "I just want to see where Conner is going. You two stay up here and wait for Manuel. When he gets back, tell him the truth—we saw a man come on board, and I'm following him."

"Okay," George agreed, "but be careful, Nancy."

"Don't worry," Nancy said. "I have my ship diagram, my flashlight, and these." She held up the set of keys to the ship.

Cautiously Nancy followed the curve of the upper deck. She heard no sound, not even footsteps. Was Conner waiting for her just around the curve? she wondered, holding her breath.

Eventually she reached the starboard side. Listening intently for sounds ahead of her, she didn't hear the footsteps behind her until it was too late.

Before she could turn, Nancy felt a hard push

in the middle of her back. She tried to grab the railing, but her fingers slipped off the slick painted wood.

In a second she had toppled over the side, plunging down toward the dark, cold waters of the Muskoka!

9

A Culprit's Confession

Gasping for breath, Nancy swam up through the icy water to the surface, about ten yards from the riverbank. Gathering her strength, she fought through the swift current until she reached a large stony ledge sticking out of the bank.

It took her last bit of energy to hoist herself up onto the ledge. She lay on her stomach, coughing and spitting out cold river water. Finally she heard George and Bess running toward her.

"Nancy!" Bess called. "Are you all right?" With her one good arm, she helped Nancy sit up.

"We heard the splash and ran around the deck in time to see you swimming toward the bank," George said. She pulled off Nancy's soaked running shoes and socks, then took off her own sweatshirt and laid it over Nancy's wet, bare feet. "How did you go overboard?"

"I was pushed," Nancy said, coughing.

"David Conner, I'll bet," Bess said.

"We can find that out later," George said. "First, you need some dry clothes, Nancy."

"There's a skirt in the trunk of my car," Nancy said, shivering. "Luckily, I didn't have time to take it to the cleaners today."

"Do you think you can make it that far?" George asked.

"If we go slow," Nancy said. Her legs wobbled when she first stood up, but she was relieved to find that she hadn't been seriously hurt.

As they walked along the riverbank, Nancy studied the *Heartliner*'s hull. "Did you see anyone aboard?" she asked George and Bess.

"No one," Bess said, "not even Manuel. I hope he's okay."

Nancy suddenly stopped. "Wait a minute," she said, pointing at the hull. "Look!"

"What do you see?" George asked.

"This is the side with the garage hold," Nancy said. "See? There are the garage doors. And there, to the right, are two more large doors. I bet they lead into another storage hold—the one off the garage hold that was walled up. Let's go back aboard and look for it." She turned and strode briskly to her car.

"Nancy, do you really think you were pushed overboard?" George asked, hurrying after her.

"Definitely," Nancy said grimly as she opened her trunk and reached for a heap of clothes.

"Then we're not going back," George said.

"It's too risky. Whoever pushed you is probably still aboard. The same person probably got Manuel out of the way and was trying to do the same to you."

"Which reminds me," Nancy said, getting into the front seat of her car to change clothes. "I should go back and try to find Manuel, too. He might need help. You can wait here if you like."

"No way," muttered Bess. "If you go, we go."

In a few minutes Nancy jumped out of the car. She was warmly dressed, but she looked ridiculous. Over a burgundy velvet skirt she wore George's worn dark green sweatshirt. She pulled the hood over her wet hair and put her running shoes back on without socks.

Bess giggled. "If the field trip kids could see you now . . ."

Returning on board the ship, the three girls stayed close together, Nancy leading the way with the diagram and the keys. Bess shuddered as they passed the room where she had had her accident. "Why would someone cut those chains and put people in such danger?" she asked.

"I don't know," Nancy said, "but I want to find out. If something has been smuggled on this ship, that could have a lot to do with it. And that long area that's sealed up behind the garage hold is a perfect hiding place."

The girls went back to the garage hold. Nothing appeared to have been moved since they had been there the previous night with Pepe and Maria.

Nancy opened the door to the small closet at the corner of the room and turned on the light. At first it looked the same as before—gray mechanics' coveralls hanging on the rod, caps and gloves on the shelf above, boots on the floor. But there was definitely something different.

Sniffing, Nancy noticed an odd smell coming from the back of the closet. It was a damp, earthy odor that she couldn't quite identify, almost like the smell in a basement. Like the rain forest pavilion at the zoo, she thought, it smelled of wet dirt and exotic animals.

Nancy pushed aside the coveralls and knelt on the floor in front of the closet. She pulled out the six grimy boots. "Careful, Nancy," Bess said. "Your beautiful skirt."

"It's on its way to the cleaners, anyway," Nancy said. "Aha!"

"What is it?" George asked, crouching next to Nancy.

"Look," Nancy said. "Down at the bottom, someone has moved one of the planks that was nailed across the back wall." On the closet floor lay a crowbar, concealed beneath the boots. The odd musty odor was stronger here, where the plank was cracked.

Nancy reached for the broken board. Suddenly she heard Bess's voice, low and trembling.

83

"N-Nancy," Bess stammered. "We have company."

Nancy whipped around, still in a crouch. She laid her hand on the crowbar, just in case she needed it for defense. Bess was standing outside the closet, and Manuel was next to her, scowling angrily.

"It is you girls!" Manuel said, lowering his flashlight as he recognized them. "Where's Pepe?"

"He couldn't come with us tonight," Nancy said.

"What a scare you gave me," Manuel said, as he took off his hat and rubbed his head. "Wait a minute. What are you doing here?" His thick, bushy black eyebrows came together as he frowned.

Nancy and George stood slowly. "I fell in the river," Nancy explained in her friendliest voice. She peeled back the sweatshirt hood to show her wet hair. "I knew there were coveralls in here, and I thought I might borrow one to change into. I promise I'll bring it back tomorrow when I come to work."

Manuel looked from Nancy, to George, to Bess. Each gave him her most winning smile. "I'm drier now, so I guess I won't be needing it after all," Nancy added. She casually closed the closet door behind her. "We couldn't find you on deck when we got here."

"I was here. I have been here at all times,"

Manuel bristled. "If I am not on deck, I am checking noises in the companionways. There is only one way on and off the ship—no one gets past me."

Nancy thought he seemed annoyed that she would question his whereabouts. She tried to disarm him with another smile.

"Now I shall escort you to the gangway," Manuel said gruffly, taking Nancy's arm. He steered them back to the gangway and watched, with his arms crossed across his chest, as Nancy, Bess, and George crossed the riverbank to Nancy's car.

Nancy took George home first, then Bess. When she reached her own home, she was glad to see her father reading in his study. He smiled at her outfit. She was still wearing George's sweatshirt, and her velvet skirt hung limp and wrinkled.

"Hmm," he said. "The uniform of the *Heartliner* hostess?"

Nancy laughed and plopped down on the sofa. "Not exactly," she answered. Briefly she told him of the adventure that she had shared with George and Bess after dinner. She tried not to dwell too much on her dunking in the Muskoka, but her father didn't let it slip by.

"Nancy, from now on I insist that you use more caution around that ship," Carson said. "It's becoming a dangerous place. Now, you go get dried off. I'll call Detective Brody and tell him what happened. I'm sure he'll want to get some people over there right away to check out the ship."

"What about the secret hold?" she asked.

"You don't know that there *is* a secret hold," Carson replied.

"But the wall," she protested, "and the boards in the closet—"

"Nancy, it's not against the law to build a wall in your own ship or to nail boards in a closet," her father pointed out. "It may not even have anything to do with the *Heartliner*'s current work. Maybe it's a layout left over from the ship's old navy days."

"Then why was it freshly painted?" she persisted.

"The ship spent two weeks in Chicago in dry dock for repairs before it came here," Mr. Drew responded. "You said that people have to back the jeeps into that garage hold. Maybe there were lots of scrapes and scratches on that wall, and it had to be painted."

"Could be," Nancy admitted. "I'll ask the nurses if they know when the wall was painted, and why. They tell me they do lots of work around the ship when it's on a mission cruise. Maybe they painted it themselves."

After giving her dad a goodnight hug, Nancy went upstairs. She was really beginning to feel the effect of her unexpected dip in the river. She was fit and a good athlete, but it had been

86

exhausting to swim fully dressed, against a current, and in water so cold.

A warm shower helped soothe her sore muscles. Dressed in her nightgown and robe, she had just curled up in bed when Hannah brought her a pot of tea and a couple of almond cookies.

"Your father said he has a message for you," the housekeeper said, fluffing up Nancy's pillows.

Despite her aching muscles, Nancy hopped out of bed and flew out of the room. She leaned over the banister on the second-floor landing. Her father looked up at her from the downstairs hall.

"I just got a phone call about the ammonium sulfide released in the dining salon on Monday," he called up the stairs to her. "Sara Lawson has just confessed!"

10

The Nasty Needles

"Sara Lawson? She confessed?" Nancy asked, stunned.

"She just called from the police station," her dad said. "She's asked me to represent her."

"But why would Nurse Lawson try to make a whole room full of children and volunteers sick to their stomachs?" Nancy wondered.

"She said she wanted to stop someone from changing the ship's missions," Mr. Drew said, shrugging. "She hoped to stop the field trips and maybe make the ship's directors cancel the cruise to the Far East."

"That doesn't make sense," Nancy said, shaking her head.

"She's staying downtown in jail tonight," Mr. Drew said, "but she'll be released on bail tomorrow morning. I'll know more after I talk to her.

Now you go to sleep. Your dunking was a shock— you need rest."

Nancy spent the next morning leading the final day's field trips in the *Heartliner*'s ICU, or Intensive Care Unit. Taking a late lunch break, at one-thirty she got in her car and drove to the Parkview Hotel, where she'd agreed to meet her dad. As she walked into the hotel's restaurant, she saw a woman sitting with her father in a private booth in the far corner. The woman's back was toward her, but Nancy recognized the bony shoulders and dark red hair of Sara Lawson.

Carson Drew stood to greet his daughter. "This is my daughter, Nancy," he told Sara. "She sometimes does research and investigative work for me. She'd like to hear your story, too, from the beginning."

Nurse Lawson scowled. "I confessed—that's it." She drank half a cup of steaming coffee in one gulp. "I emptied the vial into the pan next to the ventilation duct in the galley. I knew the fumes would spread into the air quickly, so I wore one of the gas masks from the supply hold. The smell is so bad, I knew people would leave right away and no one would really get sick. And no one did—no real harm done."

"The grand jury will decide that," Mr. Drew said. "The charges could be anything from malicious mischief to felonious assault." He took a bite of his sandwich, casually adding, "It's hard to believe that someone as devoted to the *Heartliner* as you are would do something so spiteful."

Nancy watched the nurse carefully. She knew that her best bet was just to listen and not talk.

"He's ruining the ship," Nurse Lawson said, waving her arm across her salad. "He's firing people for no good reason, stopping in ports that don't need medical care, and now this trip to the Far East . . . Why, he's even sailing his personal yacht full of bigwigs alongside the *Heartliner* part of the way. It's just showy promotion! We still have work to do in Latin America."

"Are you speaking of Dr. Diaz or Alexander Clayton?" Mr. Drew asked.

"Armando has nothing to do with this!" Nurse Lawson said, visibly upset. "It's Clayton! He treats the *Heartliner* like his second yacht."

"I understand that you have problems with the management of the ship," Mr. Drew reassured her. "But how does making dozens of schoolchildren and volunteers sick fix these problems?"

For the first time, Nancy saw Nurse Lawson's hard face soften. "It doesn't," the woman admitted. "I wanted to embarrass Clayton and call attention to what he's doing, but it was stupid. I must have been crazy."

Nancy couldn't keep quiet any longer. "Is that all there is to it? Have you done anything else this week to sabotage the ship's activities?"

"I don't know what you mean!" The nurse's face flushed a bright red. Nancy stared at her eyes behind those thick glasses, but she couldn't tell if the nurse was lying.

"Other things have happened this week that the public hasn't been told yet," Nancy said. "An elevator fell with five people inside. A bunk bed crashed down, almost crushing a student. And there's something fishy about the layout of the ship."

"Is there anything you need to tell me about what you've been doing since the luncheon on Monday?" Nancy's dad asked Lawson.

"I've been at home, at the Waterview Apartments," Lawson said, sliding out of the booth abruptly. "I know nothing about the layout of the ship or cargo or anything like that. Nothing!" Wheeling furiously, she bolted out of the room.

Nancy raised her eyebrows at her father. "That's funny," she said. "I don't recall mentioning anything about cargo."

Nancy arrived back in the *Heartliner*'s ICU ward just as a rowdy bunch of seven-year-olds filed in. As Nancy watched them tumble through the door, she felt sad, knowing that this would be her last field trip. Bess had been right—it had been fun to work as a *Heartliner* hostess.

Pepe had the children's full attention in minutes. "Here is a very special trick," he told them. "The human body is sixty-five percent water—

water that's full of minerals we need to keep us ticking. Sometimes, when people are ill, they become dehydrated—they lose too much of this water and the important minerals in it. So the doctor or nurse needs to put some fluid full of those minerals back into the patient."

He pulled a tall steel pole on wheels over to his chair in the front of the room. The students sat on beds or the floor. Nancy and Bess stood a little behind Pepe and to the side, ready to help when needed. The nurses sat at the back of the room, watching. They had told Nancy that they loved seeing Pepe do this demonstration.

At the top of Pepe's vertical pole, a steel arm stuck out at a right angle. A hook dangled from its end, and a plastic bag containing a clear liquid hung from the hook.

"The most common fluid we use is called a saline solution," Pepe continued, pointing to the plastic bag. "We start with sterile water—water that's been purified so it has no germs or bacteria —and we add sodium chloride, a chemical that you know better as salt. Then we put a needle under the skin of your arm."

Pepe paused, grinning, as the kids raised a noisy chorus of "Ugh" and "Not me—no way."

"See this tube coming out of the saline solution bag?" he continued, demonstrating as he talked. "It's called an intravenous tube. *Intra* means 'within,' and *venous* means 'vein.' Doctors like to have nicknames for everything, so we call it an IV tube. We attach it to the back of the needle—like this—and then the fluid can run through it into your body."

The kids looked at each other and smiled. A few even nodded their heads. Pepe gestured to Nancy, and she went over to a supply closet, from which she took out a large coconut.

"Now, here's the trick," Pepe said, taking the coconut from Nancy. "Look at this coconut. From the outside, it is just a hard brown fruit with three dents—like a hairy bowling ball." He waited, grinning, for the kids' laughter to stop.

"But inside, my friends, is a miracle," Pepe went on. "The liquid in a coconut is called coconut milk, but it is more like water. And it happens to be a sterile liquid—it has no germs. But what's really amazing is that it has the same amount of salt that you need for a normal IV saline solution. Watch this."

Pepe expertly opened the three holes in the coconut with an ice pick. "This opening is for the tube that goes into a patient's vein." He plugged one hole in the coconut with an IV tube.

"The second hole is used for air intake," he said. "Air flows through it into the coconut to push the fluid down through the tube.

"This last opening is a bonus," Pepe went on. "If you need another medicine, we can put it into the coconut with a second tube here. Then the medicine will flow down the IV tube into your body also." Pepe juggled the tubes around to show the intake and outflow.

The children clapped and whistled when Pepe finished. Nancy and Pepe took the IV pole and the coconut to the supply closet, and Bess went to the front of the room.

"You may have heard of blood banks," Bess said, following a set of notes that had been written out for the volunteers. "They are places where people donate small amounts of their own blood. The blood is then stored, just like money in a regular bank. When other people lose blood during an operation or in an accident, they can get more from the blood bank."

Nancy lay down on a bed and rolled up the sleeve of her sweater. Pepe motioned the children to gather around the table so they could watch.

"The places where the *Heartliner* goes have no blood banks," Bess continued. "So the *Heartliner* doctors and nurses start up blood banks in those areas. The staff and crew of the ship give blood to stock the bank. Nancy will show you how."

Some of the children crowded forward to see. Others hung back, hiding their eyes, then peeking.

Pepe tied a thin elastic tube above Nancy's elbow. "This is called a tourniquet," he said. "See that blue ridge in Nancy's arm? That's her vein—a tube in the body that carries blood around.

"The tourniquet makes the vein stand out so that we can get a needle into it," he explained. "Clench your fist a couple of times, Nancy—that gets the blood flowing well."

Pepe wiped Nancy's skin with a cotton ball dipped in alcohol. A sudden stir at the door made everyone turn.

Nancy was startled to see Dr. Diaz come into the room. He walked quickly to the bed where she was lying. "I'll finish the demonstration," he said brusquely to Pepe. The students fell silent. Dr. Diaz's manner was stiff, unlike Pepe's exciting presentation.

Dr. Diaz began to speak, describing the tube and the bag in which the blood would be collected. As she listened, Nancy watched Pepe pick up a sealed packet containing a new sterile needle. She saw the side of the packet flap open and the needle fall to the floor.

Pepe picked up the needle, looked at it, and frowned. Nancy watched him riffle hastily through the rest of the packets in the box. Then, with a sideways glance at Dr. Diaz, Pepe tiptoed over to the supply closet and took out a new box of needles. He opened it and handed a sealed packet to Dr. Diaz, who was just finishing his lecture.

Dr. Diaz deftly inserted the needle into

Nancy's vein and began to draw her blood. As she lay on the bed with the tube in her arm, Nancy watched Pepe take the first box of needles and slip out of the room.

Dr. Diaz finished the demonstration and left, with a cold nod to the students. The field trip was over, and the nurses led the students out.

Bess brought Nancy a glass of orange juice to help her restore the fluid in her body after giving blood. "That sure was odd," Bess said while Nancy sipped her juice. "I wonder why Maria's dad butted in like that. And where did Pepe go?"

As if on cue, Pepe walked back in just then. He was carrying the original box of needles and a small book. His usual grin had been replaced with a grim look.

"What is it, Pepe?" Nancy asked.

"This might have been a very unlucky day for you," he said in a grave voice.

Pepe opened the book and showed Nancy a picture of a large gray snake. A pattern of pale diamonds bordered in black covered its skin. Its chin was yellow, and the caption read: "Barba amarilla (also known as fer-de-lance or lancehead), an extremely venomous pit viper."

"These needles, Nancy," Pepe said, pointing to the syringes. "The tips have been dipped in something. I am afraid it is the venom of the barba amarilla!"

11

Strange Stowaways

Nancy gulped. If it hadn't been for Pepe's cool thinking, she would have been poisoned!

"I thought it was strange that the first syringe packet opened so easily," Pepe explained. "Then I saw that the needles in this box had been tampered with—they'd been opened and resealed.

"I took the whole box down to the pathology lab. The microscope there is very good," he went on. "When I looked at the needles under the microscope, I saw a sticky yellow goo on the tips. Only an expert can tell for sure, but I recognize the smell of that stuff. I think it is the venom of the barba amarilla!"

"Barbara Ann?" Bess asked, puzzled.

"No, barba amarilla—it's Spanish for yellow beard," Pepe said. "Because their chins are yellow, see?" He pointed to the picture again.

Taking the book with them, Nancy and Bess followed Pepe to the pathology lab, where a microscope was set up on a lab table. The girls took turns leaning over and looking at the needle Pepe had laid under the powerful lens. They could see the yellow residue on the tip.

"It is a terrible poison," Pepe said, his eyes dark.

Trembling, Bess sat down hard in the chair behind her. "Nancy, what if—"

"We have antivenin on board—it's a medicine that neutralizes poison from many tropical insects and vipers, including barba amarilla," Pepe said, motioning to the cabinet on the wall. "Antivenin works wonders if the victim receives it in time. But with the venom concealed as it was on this needle, we wouldn't have realized that there *was* poison involved. We might not have figured it out in time to give you the antivenin."

He looked at Nancy and shook his head. She felt faint, frightened by her close brush with danger.

Then a surge of determination revived her. "Come on," she said. "We have to get these needles to the police." Picking up a roll of surgical tape from the table, she began to seal up the box of suspicious syringe packets.

Suddenly she heard a footstep in the doorway behind her. "What are you three doing here?"

Nancy turned to see Armando Diaz at the lab

door. "I thought the field trips were over for the day," he said, frowning. "What do you have in that box?"

Before Nancy could stop him, Pepe earnestly told Dr. Diaz what he had discovered. The doctor became more and more distressed as Pepe talked. When Pepe told him what he suspected was on the needle, Dr. Diaz cried out. "No, it couldn't be! Let me see it."

"The box is sealed, Dr. Diaz," Nancy said, grabbing the box. "I'm taking it to the police."

"I'm chief of staff here, and I'll check the syringes myself," Dr. Diaz said in a tight voice. "If anything should be taken to the police, I'll do it." He held out his hand.

Nancy stood still, hugging the box.

"Nancy, that is *Heartliner* property." Dr. Diaz's voice grew harsher. "Please give it to me now." Nancy had no choice. Dr. Diaz took the box from her hands and walked out.

Pepe was very quiet as he put the microscope away. Nancy chewed her lip, silently trying to make sense of Dr. Diaz's behavior. Why wouldn't he let her take the suspicious syringes to Detective Brody? Did he really want to check the needles? Or was he going to alter the evidence— or even worse, destroy it?

Nancy's thoughts were interrupted by George's voice. "Nancy! Bess! Where are you? They're closing the ship."

99

Popping her head out the door, Bess motioned George and Maria into the lab. Pepe closed the door after them. Quickly Bess told the other two girls what had happened in the intensive care unit. Nancy then recounted the scene with Dr. Diaz.

Maria looked very upset when she heard what her father had done. "Why would he take the needles?" she cried. "Why didn't he let you take them to the police?"

Bess put her good arm around Maria's shoulders. "Please, Maria, I know it looks bad. But we'll think of something, won't we, Nancy?"

Everyone turned to look at Nancy. She looked at the circle of friends. Sweet, loyal Bess. Strong, outspoken George. Pepe, who may have saved her life. And Maria, miserable and frantic. They were all counting on her.

Nancy thought back over the day's activities and remembered one more baffling player in this mystery—David Conner. "Has anyone seen David Conner today?" she asked.

"I haven't seen him since last night on the ship, before you were dunked," Bess said.

"I usually see him hanging around the press tent before we board or during breaks," George put in. "But not today."

"I haven't seen him either," Nancy said. She stepped over to the lab's phone and dialed the Riverview Suites Hotel. The desk clerk rang Conner's room, but there was no answer.

"He hasn't checked out, then?" Nancy asked the clerk.

"No," the clerk replied. "But he does have several messages waiting for him. It looks like he hasn't stopped by to pick them up since yesterday afternoon."

After Nancy hung up the phone, she told her friends what she had learned.

"We never saw him leave the ship last night," George noted.

"Maybe he didn't leave," Bess said in a nervous voice. "Maybe he's still on the ship."

"If he was here all night, he could have doctored those needles," Maria pointed out.

Nancy's brain raced. She still had Maria's set of keys. Maybe she could find David Conner's hiding place!

She checked her watch. It was five minutes until six. In five minutes the staff would lock up the *Heartliner* for the day. Since this was the final day of the field trips, they would no doubt make an extra careful sweep of the ship.

"I have a feeling that the answers to a lot of our questions lie in the garage hold," Nancy said. "I've got to get in there tonight. Pepe, where would be a good place to hide while Manuel and the nurses lock up the ship?"

Pepe considered the question for a minute, then his eyes lit up. "The dental clinic!" he exclaimed. "There have been no field trips scheduled there this week. Since it hasn't been used, it probably hasn't been unlocked. I'll bet that Manuel doesn't even check inside there when he locks up the rest of the ship."

"Point the way, Pepe," Nancy said eagerly. "And hurry!"

One by one, they darted across the hall to the stairway. Then they ran down the steps as fast and as quietly as they could. When they reached the middle deck, Pepe opened the stairwell door a crack, peeked through, then rapidly shut the door again. He motioned for everyone to crouch down so they wouldn't be seen through the window at the top of the door.

They could hear a couple of nurses coming down the companionway, rattling door handles to make sure they were locked. The nurses' voices stopped by the elevator, right on the other side of the door from the stairwell.

"Boy, Dr. Diaz sure was cranky today," one nurse was saying.

"He's been a real bear for weeks," the other nurse agreed. "I hope he lightens up before we set sail for the Far East, or it'll be a long trip."

Nancy saw Pepe take Maria's hand and give it a reassuring squeeze.

Crouching in the stairwell, the five friends listened as the elevator doors opened and then closed again. Nancy cautiously opened the door and peeked out. The nurses were gone. "All clear," she whispered.

Pepe led the girls down the companionway to a

room at the far end. Nancy checked the set of keys until she found the one labeled Dental Clinic.

Pepe stood guard watching one direction, George the other, as Nancy fit the key in the lock. "Someone's coming!" George whispered. "I hear footsteps!"

Nancy felt the lock slip and swiftly turned the knob. She threw open the door, and the five friends scrambled into the dark room. Nancy quietly pushed the door shut, then turned the lock. She didn't turn on the light, knowing that it would shine out under the door.

Two sets of footsteps came closer and closer. Finally they stopped just on the other side of the door. Only two inches of metal separated Nancy and her friends from the people in the companionway.

Someone on the other side of the door tried the handle. Once. Twice. There was a moment of silence. Then the footsteps began again and the people in the companionway moved on.

Bess put her hand over her heart. Maria's back slid down the wall until she sat on the floor.

They waited for what seemed hours, though it was only thirty minutes by Nancy's glow-in-the-dark watch face. Little by little, their eyes adapted to the dark. Nancy could make out furniture, a dentist's chair, other equipment, and sinks and cupboards.

At last Nancy whispered through the dark to

her friends. "It's seven o'clock now—I guess it might be safe to leave the room."

"Thank goodness," Bess sighed, relieved.

Nancy groped over to the door and opened it. She carefully looked out, then motioned them all to follow her.

The main lights inside the ship had been turned off, but a dim glow was cast by pale green light bulbs, set every several yards along the companionway ceiling. Nancy and her friends returned to the stairwell and headed for the lower deck. They ran to the end of the companionway. Nancy unlocked the door to the garage hold, and they went inside.

Nancy walked straight over to the closet in the newly painted wall. Again she pushed aside the hanging coveralls and dragged out the boots.

There were still some planks nailed crisscross over the back of the closet, but more had been yanked out. The sweet earthy odor she'd smelled before was stronger than ever.

Nancy quickly found a crowbar and a flashlight in a stack of mechanic's tools in the hold. George and Pepe helped her pry and pull at the planks. Soon there was a hole in the back of the closet big enough to crawl through. Beyond the hole yawned blackness.

Nancy climbed through the hole first, switching on the flashlight. George followed, and then Maria.

"I don't want to go in there," Bess said, "but I

don't want to stay out here alone, either!'' Pepe helped her through the opening, being careful of her arm in the sling. Then he followed her in.

Nancy flashed her electric beam into the darkness. It was a long room, the same length as the other room across the companionway, the one with all the machinery in it. Down the left side, hundreds of unmarked brown cardboard boxes were stacked from floor to ceiling, several layers deep.

Then Nancy heard a funny sound on her right-hand side—low and faint, sort of like a whispered whistle. For some reason, it made the hair on the back of her neck bristle.

She swung the flashlight around toward the noise. Following the light with their eyes, everyone gasped.

The right-hand wall was stacked with metal mesh cages. In each cage wriggled two bright green lizards, their hot pink tongues flicking eerily in and out.

"Oh, no, Nancy!'' Bess shrieked. "It's a whole roomful of them—the Barbara Ann snakes! We have to get out of here!''

12

A Secret Life

"Hush, Bess," Nancy said. "These aren't those poisonous snakes, are they, Pepe?"

"No," he said. "The barba amarilla is a snake, Bess. These, as you can see, are not."

"Well, they're creepy and crawly, and that's enough for me," Bess declared.

"Do you know what they are, Pepe?" Nancy asked. She flashed her light toward the creatures inside the cages, and he took a closer look.

"*Sí*. They look like a lizard that I have seen up in the hills behind my village," he said. "I don't know their exact name. Some call them *lengua fresa*, which means 'strawberry tongue.'"

"Yellow chin, strawberry tongue," George commented. "Beautiful names for these creatures."

"You seem pretty calm about these lizards,

106

Pepe," Nancy said. "I take it they're not dangerous."

"They do not bite or sting," he answered. "However, they can be a problem if you eat them."

"Eat them! Ugh!" Bess said.

"Some people do," Pepe insisted. "They're very sweet, I hear."

"There you go, Bess," George said. "A new diet delight!"

"Unfortunately, you may pay dearly for the sweet taste," Pepe explained. "Some people have bad allergic reactions from eating lenguas fresas. They become very ill, and they may be partly paralyzed. They can even lose their hearing or their eyesight."

"How dreadful," George said. "Why would there be so many of them aboard the *Heartliner?*"

"Not for any good reason, I suspect," Nancy said, "or they wouldn't be hidden down here. I wonder what's in these boxes?" She walked down the long dark room, flashing the light along the stacks of cartons on the left-hand wall. The others followed her, trying to stay near the only light in the room. The lenguas fresas kept up their haunting chorus of whistles and sighs.

About halfway down the room, the group came upon a large trash barrel bolted to the wall. Inside were a few large tin cans. Their sides were badly bashed in, as though they'd been dropped

107

during loading. Where a couple of cans had broken open, some tan powder had spilled out over the bottom of the trash barrel.

"Maria," Nancy said, "may I have your scarf?"

"Sure," Maria answered. She untied the turquoise and purple scarf she had draped around her shoulders.

Nancy carefully used the scarf to protect her hands as she picked up one of the split cans of powder. She wrapped the can and its spilled contents tightly in the scarf.

With her flashlight, Nancy finished inspecting the storage space. There was nothing there besides the brown boxes and the cages of lizards. Together, the five friends went back to the concealed entrance to the secret hold.

They crawled back through the hole in the closet. Nancy and George held the planks in place while Pepe pushed the nails back into the holes with the crowbar. It seemed very quiet, now that they couldn't hear the hissing lizards.

"Pepe, do you know Manuel's routine?" Nancy asked. "Last night he told us that he's always at his post unless he's checking on noises. But he seemed angry when he said it. Maybe he felt guilty because he wasn't where he should have been last night."

Pepe shrugged. "I always see him just sitting in his chair by the gangway. Once he has made his rounds with the nurses at lock-up time, I bet he does not leave that chair. The gangway is the only way anyone can enter the ship, so all he has to do is keep an eye on it."

"That doesn't give us much of a chance to get off the ship," Nancy said wryly.

"I can divert him," Pepe said, eyes sparkling with fun. "Let me talk Manuel out of his chair, and you all can leave the ship."

Nancy smiled. "You're on! We'll wait near the gangway. You signal when the coast is clear."

Pepe nodded. "When you hear me sing, run for the gangway."

The four girls hid in the companionway just off the main deck. Nancy felt against her leg the heavy can she'd wrapped up in Maria's scarf.

Pepe walked out onto the deck. Nancy heard his lilting voice say, "Ah, Manuel, *mi amigo.*"

"Hey, Pepe!" Manuel's voice showed that he was surprised to see the young man. "When did you come on board? How did you sneak past me?"

"I have been here all day, my friend, studying," Pepe said, sounding very sincere. "Now I am ready to go. But you, Manuel, you work hard, too—you deserve a break, no? How about some *café con leche*—coffee with milk? I know where there are some cookies in the galley."

"Well, I am on duty. . . ." Manuel hesitated.

"Come and keep me company while I make us a treat," Pepe wheedled.

There was a moment of silence. Then the girls heard Pepe's voice break out in a rousing chorus of "Take Me Out to the Ball Game."

The song faded as Pepe led Manuel down to the galley. Nancy peeked around the doorway, then motioned the girls to follow her. They ran across the deck, down the gangway, and across the riverbank to the parking lot. They waited for Pepe by their cars.

Pepe joined them in fifteen minutes. "I found out what happened to Manuel last night," he said excitedly. "He got a phone call from Riverside Hospital from someone who said he was calling for your father, Maria. He said that Dr. Diaz wanted Manuel to come to the hospital at once—something about an emergency."

Pepe took a huge breath. "But when he got to the doctor's office, it was closed. Dr. Diaz was gone, and no one knew anything about the call."

"Maybe David Conner called Manuel to lure him away, so Conner could sneak onto the ship," Maria suggested.

"I bet Conner's the one who's been cutting bed chains and poisoning needles," Bess declared. "Every time something bad happens, he's around—except today, and we're not sure about that."

"I think we'll know more when we find out what this stuff is," Nancy said, holding up Maria's scarf. "For now, I suggest we all go home and get a good night's sleep."

* * *

The next day was Friday. Nancy woke up early and pulled on jeans and a yellow sweater. She knew that today was her last chance to find out the truth about the *Heartliner*. The field trips for the children were finished. A last few VIP tours had been scheduled for that morning. All afternoon the ship would be bustling with preparations for Alexander Clayton's testimonial dinner. And after the banquet, late that night, the *Heartliner* would set sail for the Far East.

She grabbed her canvas backpack. It already contained the copies of the cruise records that Maria had found. Now she put in a plastic bag containing the can of powder wrapped in Maria's scarf. Then she headed for Riverview College and the office of Jane Firestone, a chemistry professor who was a friend of the Drew family.

Jane was a tall woman with short brown hair and a big smile. "Lizards, hmmm?" she said, after Nancy had told her about the previous night's discoveries.

"Sounds pretty weird, doesn't it?" Nancy said. "Maybe this is lizard food." Carefully, she pulled the can out of Maria's bright scarf.

"I'll start checking the powder out right away," Jane said, rubbing a pinch of it curiously between her fingertips. "I can't promise anything, but I may be able to rule out a few possibilities. Give me a call after noon."

Next Nancy went to the police station to talk to Detective Brody. The desk sergeant told her that

Brody was out for the day, but that Nancy could probably catch him at the Clayton testimonial dinner that evening.

"One more question," Nancy said. "Do you know if a Dr. Armando Diaz brought in some evidence yesterday afternoon? A packet of poisoned syringes?"

The sergeant frowned as he glanced through the desk log. "Sorry, he never came by. It would be written down here if he did."

After thanking the sergeant, Nancy walked out of the station house. Stopping by a newsstand just outside, she bought a copy of the River Heights *Morning Record*. The headlines were all about Sara Lawson and the smelly gas on the *Heartliner*.

If something is being smuggled, Nancy wondered, is Nurse Lawson involved? Or is she trying to protect someone, like Dr. Diaz?

Nancy decided to try to talk to Sara. She drove over to Cottage Street and the Waterview Apartments, where Sara had said she lived.

The apartments were in a high-rise pink brick building that wrapped around a courtyard with a small fountain. Nancy found the nurse's name on the mailbox for apartment 8B. She took the elevator to the eighth floor.

Nancy walked down the hall and knocked on the door of apartment 8B. There was no answer. She knocked again, harder, but still no one responded. She finally left, frustrated.

By the time Nancy reached home, it was a

quarter past eleven, and Hannah was preparing lunch. Nancy found her father on the terrace, reading the same newspaper she had just bought.

"What a treat," Nancy said. "My busy dad came home for lunch!"

"I came home to bring you big news." Mr. Drew sighed, folding up his newspaper. His face was serious and his eyes looked sad.

"Your suspicions were right, Nancy," he told her. "There is a secret in Armando Diaz's past—a very dark one, indeed!"

13

Formula for Danger

"Oh no, Dad," Nancy said. "So Dr. Diaz *does* have something he's trying to keep quiet."

Carson Drew nodded heavily. "My friend called this morning from California. He said that nineteen years ago, Armando Diaz arrived from Brazil and started working at San Diego Mercury Hospital. He knew no one in this country. He hadn't even met his future wife, Francesca."

"Was he on staff there?" Nancy asked.

"Yes, but he hadn't graduated from an American medical school and didn't have an American medical license, so he worked as an associate," Mr. Drew answered. "To get his full position, he had to pass a foreign medical graduates exam, then get his California state medical license.

"Shortly after he started working in the emergency room trauma center," he continued, "a patient died under mysterious circumstances."

114

"Was it his fault?" Nancy asked uneasily.

"Apparently not—officially," her dad said, patting her hand. "There was an investigation and the medical staff was cleared. But several nasty newspaper articles cast the blame on him—a new young doctor, and a foreigner."

"It must have been so hard on Dr. Diaz." Nancy sighed. "Alone in a new country, excited about his new career—and then disaster."

They both looked up as Hannah brought out their lunch: homemade tomato soup and roast beef sandwiches on crusty rye bread.

"So what happened after the investigation?" Nancy asked. "Was Dr. Diaz fired or anything?"

"No," Mr. Drew said. "Armando was well liked at the hospital. The administration supported him a hundred percent. But I guess he still felt bad about it. He left San Diego, without a word, a few days after the investigation was closed."

"Where did he go?" Nancy asked, chomping on a crisp dill pickle.

"My friend never knew," he answered. "Then ten years later, he heard that Dr. Diaz had gotten the position at Riverside. He tried to contact him, but Armando never answered his phone calls."

"Maybe Dr. Diaz wanted to put that part of his life behind him for good," Nancy suggested.

"Could be." Her dad paused to try the soup. "And here's one more odd thing. While checking on Armando, my friend couldn't find any evidence that he ever took the foreign medical graduates exam, or the licensing tests of any state."

"What!" Nancy said. "Isn't it illegal for him to practice medicine without a license?"

"Yes," Mr. Drew said, "but it happens. Once a doctor has established his career, people just assume he has a license. No one bothers to check."

"Poor Maria," Nancy said. "She's really going to be upset by all this. I'm sure she doesn't know." She pushed her plate aside. "Dad, suppose that someone found all this out and blackmailed Dr. Diaz?"

Mr. Drew considered the possibility. "I can imagine that he might do almost anything to cover this up. If the truth got out . . . well, he could practice medicine again, after he took the licensing test. But it would be extremely embarrassing, for him and for the *Heartliner*."

"And it would hurt the *Heartliner*'s efforts to raise money, I'll bet," Nancy added.

"Right," her father said. "And I hear that Francesca Diaz is in line to be appointed as a judge. Armando might be afraid that if the truth about his background came out, it would hurt her chances. He may be protecting her, too."

Nancy checked her watch. It was almost twelve-thirty. She gave her father a quick kiss on the forehead, grabbed her backpack, and raced from the terrace to her car.

Nancy drove back to the river. Before visiting Jane Firestone's office, she decided she'd try another stop at Sara Lawson's apartment. Turning into the Waterview complex again, she parked her car, got out, and went inside the pink highrise. She went to apartment 8B and rang the bell.

When Nurse Lawson opened her door, she was startled to see Nancy. For a second it looked as if she were going to slam the door in her face. Instead she sighed, asking, "What do you want?"

"I want to talk to you," Nancy said. "I won't take much of your time. It's important."

Nurse Lawson stiffly moved aside to let her in. They stood awkwardly in the apartment's tiny entry hall.

"Nurse Lawson, you got very upset when you thought my father and I were criticizing Dr. Diaz," Nancy said.

"I told you, none of the problems with the ship have anything to do with him," Lawson said.

"But how do you know?" Nancy asked. "I have reason to believe Dr. Diaz may not be all he says he is. There may be some issues in his past—"

"Who told you that?" Nurse Lawson cried. "You can't believe those vicious rumors. They're lies, I tell you—lies!"

"What lies?" Nancy asked. "Are you talking about the incident in San Diego?"

Nurse Lawson looked at Nancy, stunned. She nodded her head slowly. "No one here knows about that," she said. "Not even his wife. I recently found out from a nurse in San Diego. I confronted Armando about it, but he swore me to secrecy until he can tell Francesca. He said he wants to be the one to tell Alexander Clayton, too."

"I know you don't like Clayton," Nancy said.

"I certainly don't," the nurse said.

"You mentioned that he had fired people," Nancy stated. "Were you talking about the crew in Buenos Aires?"

"Exactly," Nurse Lawson said. "Those people were dumped for no good reason. Everything was running smoothly. Suddenly Clayton flew down to meet the ship, fired thirty-one men, and installed all new people. Then the *Heartliner* sailed to San Rafael, Argentina, where no medical care was needed. It wasn't until Clayton flew back to the States that we got on with our mission."

"What did the staff do the two days you were in San Rafael?" Nancy asked.

"What we always do in a new port," the nurse said. "We formed medical teams to go out into the surrounding area, looking for people to help. We held seminars and taught new medical procedures to the local doctors and nurses."

"Did Dr. Diaz go out with you into the countryside?" Nancy asked.

"As a matter of fact, no," Lawson answered. "He stayed on board with Clayton the whole time. Armando really hasn't been the same since."

118

"One last question," Nancy said, watching the woman closely. "When we met the last time, with my father, you said you didn't know anything about the ship's odd layout or about cargo. I never mentioned cargo, Nurse Lawson. Why did you?"

The nurse reluctantly met Nancy's stare. "There were rumors in San Rafael that the *Heartliner* was taking on or dumping a large cargo load. But when I asked Armando about it, he ordered me out of the room."

"Have you ever been in the large cargo holds on the lowest deck?" Nancy asked.

Nurse Lawson looked puzzled. "I've been in the garage hold often, to get the jeeps," she said. "But I have no idea of any other hold."

Thanking the nurse, Nancy left quickly. She was convinced Lawson had told her all she knew.

Nancy hurried quickly to Jane Firestone's office. When she walked in, the chemist looked up excitedly. "I've got more answers than I expected," she greeted Nancy. "I can't be positive until I actually have one of those little lizards in my hands. But take a look at this."

She picked up a folder from her desk. It was full of articles about dangerous and illegal diet products—liquids, tablets, and powders.

"The powder in the can you brought me has the same formula as this." Jane pointed to an article on a preparation called KalorieKill. "An unfortunate name, I'm afraid," she added.

119

Nancy skimmed the article quickly. This particular formula had been introduced in Europe and the Far East two years earlier. It was very successful, though nothing in it was proven to help people lose weight.

But there were potentially lethal side effects, the article went on—paralysis or blindness. The product had been taken off the market. It couldn't be manufactured, imported, or sold in America. But it was still sold illegally in Europe, the Far East, and the Middle East.

Looking up, Nancy murmured. "Paralysis or blindness? Pepe said that people who eat that lizard have the same bad effects."

"Exactly!" Jane said. "There's an enzyme in this diet formula that I'll bet comes from your wiggly green friends. I sure would like to have a lizard to check out."

Nancy sifted through the other articles. All were about dangerous diet preparations and how they often hurt people's health.

Then the author's name jumped out at her from the page: David Conner, reporter for the Washington *Investigative Journal!*

"Can I take these lab results and some of these newspaper articles with me?" Nancy asked. Jane nodded, and Nancy stuffed them into her backpack with her other evidence.

Using Jane's phone, Nancy called Bess and asked her to meet her at George's house. By the time Nancy pulled up at the Faynes', both girls

120

were waiting on the front lawn. They jumped into the Mustang and Nancy drove away.

As they headed toward the *Heartliner*, Nancy briefed them quickly about Dr. Diaz's past. Then she told them what Jane had said about the powder from the secret hold.

"So how is that connected with the machinery in the other hold?" Bess wondered. "You know, the conveyor belt and the big copper kettles."

"Maybe that equipment was used to manufacture the diet formula," Nancy guessed. "And the lizards are the raw material."

"But what's it all doing on the *Heartliner*?" Bess looked confused.

"Remember, the formula is illegal," Nancy said, steering into a parking space across from the hospital ship. "Pretend you're the owner of the plant, and you learn that the authorities are closing in on you. You're making so much money, you don't want to close it for good—you just want to relocate.

"So you find a big ship that happens to be in the area," she continued. "You dismantle your factory, put it all on the ship, and take it to—"

"River Heights?" George put in, perplexed.

"Only for a week, George," Nancy said with a smile. "Your final destination is the Far East!"

"Oh, Nancy," Bess said, breathlessly. "Does that mean that Maria's dad *is* involved?"

"I have no idea," Nancy said. "Anyway, this is just a theory. That's why we have to get one of

121

those lizards and take it to Jane. Once she makes a positive identification of the powder, then we can present our evidence to the police."

"Oh, no," Bess moaned, looking up at the ship. "I can't go in that dark old hold again."

"We've got to, Bess," Nancy said firmly. She checked her watch. "It's a quarter to three—the banquet's at seven. We'll have enough time."

Lots of people were on board the *Heartliner*—caterers, florists, and party decorators. No one paid any attention to Nancy and her friends. They took the elevator to the lowest deck, used Maria's keys once more, and were quickly in the garage hold. Nancy locked the door behind them and turned on the light.

"That's odd," she noted, looking around. "One of the jeeps is missing."

Shrugging, she headed for the closet. Bess and George followed her. Finding the crowbar again, Nancy and George pulled out the boards nailed across the back wall. Leaving Bess behind as a lookout, they slipped through the hole into the secret hold.

Nancy turned on the flashlight. She and George gasped at the same time.

The secret hold was empty!

14

Walking the Plank

"I don't believe it!" Nancy said, her words a whisper. George just stood and stared.

"What's going on?" Bess wailed from the other side of the wall. "Why are you so quiet? Just grab a lizard and let's get out of here."

"Shhh," George said. "We'll be right back."

Nancy and George ran down to the end of the room. The flashlight beam bounced along the walls, the floor, and the ceiling. Their footsteps echoed in the emptiness.

At the end of the room, George turned to go back. An odd sparkle caught Nancy's eye. There in the corner something glittered.

She reached down and picked it up. It was a gold coin etched with an anchor that had been made into a man's tie tack. It looked familiar to Nancy, and she slipped it into her jeans pocket.

She and George rejoined Bess, and together

they left the garage hold. Nancy dashed across the companionway to the matching hold on the other side. "I'll bet they've moved all the factory equipment, too," she said, searching the ring for the other hold's key. She found it and fit it into the lock. "Hmmm, that's funny," she murmured. "The key doesn't work."

She crouched down and examined the door. "It looks as if they changed the lock," she groaned. "See how the paint's all scratched around the cylinder?"

Frustrated, Nancy, Bess, and George headed back to the upper deck. "Ooooh, look," Bess said, pointing over the railing. "There's the *Seafarer*—Alexander Clayton's yacht."

Bobbing against another pontoon dock fifty yards upriver was a gleaming white yacht, trimmed with mellow teakwood and sparkling brass.

"Sara Lawson told me that Clayton and a few VIP guests would be sailing alongside the *Heartliner* for the first leg of its journey," Nancy remembered. "That's probably why the yacht's moored here now. I bet they'll go on board right after the banquet and sail away."

She checked her watch again. "Speaking of the banquet, what time are we hostesses supposed to meet here to help with the banquet?"

"At a quarter past six," Bess answered. "Guests will start arriving around six-thirty. The hos-

tesses are supposed to guide people around and seat them."

"Okay, it's almost four o'clock," Nancy said. "I need you to do me a big favor, Bess. Can you drive?"

Bess moved her arm tentatively within her sling. "I think so, Nancy," she said. "I'll try."

"I want you to take my car, go home, and get ready for this evening," Nancy said. "Then go to George's house and my house and pick up our stuff for tonight. George, make a list of what you want Bess to bring back." She pulled a pad of paper and a pen from her backpack. When George finished, Nancy added her list.

"George and I are going to see Dr. Diaz at the hospital," Nancy explained to Bess. "I'm going to tell him what I know and see what he says. We'll meet you back in the ship's classroom about five-thirty. We'll change then."

Bess beamed. "You can count on me, Nancy," she said. Nancy smiled, knowing it was true. Even though Bess complained a lot, she would always be there when Nancy needed her.

Nancy and George headed across the riverbank as Bess drove off. Within minutes, they were inside the hospital, following the green line on the floor to the South Wing.

As they approached Dr. Diaz's office, they were surprised to hear loud, angry voices. Nancy recognized one as Dr. Diaz's, and the other as

Alexander Clayton's. She motioned to George to stay still while they listened.

"I won't do it, Alexander," Nancy heard Dr. Diaz say irritably. "Nothing you can say will change my mind now."

"Armando, you're not thinking clearly," Clayton's mellow voice reasoned. "I've protected you so far, and I'll continue to do so. But only as long as you keep your end of the bargain."

Dr. Diaz mumbled something that Nancy couldn't hear, then Clayton spoke again, softly. Nancy strained to hear him say, "Just think of your family. Think of the *Heartliner*. Everything in your life could be destroyed in an instant."

Nancy reached her hand into her jeans pocket, and clasped the gold tie tack. Of course! Alexander Clayton was behind everything!

Nancy grabbed George's arm and pulled her back along the green line to the hospital lobby. When they were out on the lawn, she finally spoke.

"Look," she said, pulling out the tie tack. "I found this in the secret hold. I'm sure it's Clayton's. While we were listening to him argue with Dr. Diaz, I was picturing him in my mind. I imagined him wearing what he wore Saturday to the meeting at Maria's—and it was this tie tack and matching cuff links!"

"Why would Alexander Clayton be in a hold full of lizards and diet powder?" George asked.

"Come on," Nancy said. "If I'm right, we have

126

less than twelve hours to stop this illegal cargo from being smuggled out of town."

Nancy sprinted toward the *Seafarer,* Clayton's yacht, and George followed closely.

From behind a truck parked along the riverbank, Nancy surveyed the scene. She could see a young man on board the yacht, polishing a large brass bell that hung over the forward deck.

"You go distract him," Nancy whispered to George. "Talk about sailing or something."

"What are you going to do?" George whispered back.

"I'm going aboard the yacht to see if I can find some answers," Nancy said.

"Okay, but be careful!" George said. She stepped out from behind the truck and strolled onto the dock. Nancy could hear her strike up a conversation with the young man. She waited until George had maneuvered him into the pilot's cabin.

While George and the man looked at the yacht's gauges and dials, Nancy scurried along the dock, up the short ramp onto the yacht, and down into the salon. She wasn't sure what she was looking for, but she knew she needed something to link Clayton to the smuggled cargo.

The salon was a large elegant room, complete with billiard table and crystal chandelier. Nancy prowled about, checking out drawers and cabinets. She found no evidence of any illegal manufacturing business.

Knowing that George couldn't distract the crewman for too long, Nancy hurried into the galley. She checked every drawer and cabinet but found nothing unusual.

Then she opened the refrigerator, and she shuddered. There, lying on a shelf on its back, was a lengua fresa. Its eyes were closed.

Grabbing a dishcloth, Nancy gingerly picked up the lizard by the very tip of its tail. She wrapped its stiff, ten-inch-long body in the towel, then jammed it into her backpack.

She tiptoed back through the salon and up the steps onto the deck. As she stepped forward, suddenly a hand grabbed her shoulder!

A large, mean-looking man spun her around roughly. He wore khaki workpants and a long-sleeved denim shirt.

"Hey, Bart!" he called out. "Look what I found. You suppose this is her little friend?"

The young man George had been talking to poked his head out of the pilot's cabin. Nancy saw him shove George out onto the deck in front of him. "Now what do we do, Wayne?" Bart said.

The big man—Wayne—pushed Nancy and George back into the salon. He whipped out a length of twine and tied their hands behind them. The position was awkward for Nancy because of her backpack. She could feel the large cold lizard like a lump against her back.

Wayne forced them down onto a leather sofa.

"Watch 'em, Bart," he growled to his companion. "I'll find out what to do and be right back."

Nancy saw Wayne go into the galley, dial the phone, and mutter into it. Then he hung up and came back to the salon. "Get the jeep and open the hold again," he ordered Bart. "We're going back to the ship."

Bart left and Wayne stood in the salon doorway, watching. In a few minutes he waved, turned around, and pulled Nancy and George to their feet. He marched them off the yacht to a jeep parked at the end of the dock.

"Don't make a sound," Wayne muttered behind them as he guided them to the car, "or you'll go back in the river, this time for good." Nancy felt his right hand clamped harshly on her arm.

Glancing around, Nancy saw no hope of help. The *Seafarer* was moored well away from the medical ship. No traffic drove this far up the riverbank, and the nearest warehouses were boarded up.

Bart stood by the jeep with the back door open. Wayne shoved Nancy and George onto the backseat floor. Nancy wriggled around so that her backpack wouldn't be crushed.

"You two better stay still," grunted Wayne. Then he flung a canvas cloth over them.

The engine started, and the jeep bumped over the riverbank's rough pavement. Within minutes, the jeep stopped, swerved, then went into reverse.

As the back of the car angled upward, Nancy and George tumbled against the back of the front seat. The jeep inched backward. Nancy guessed they were going up a ramp into the garage hold's side doors.

Finally the jeep leveled out, and then it stopped. Wayne yanked off the canvas, and Nancy looked out. She recognized the tan walls and piles of auto equipment. They were back in the garage hold of the *Heartliner*.

George gave Nancy a startled stare. Nancy flashed back a "keep quiet" look.

While Bart closed the doors, Wayne pushed Nancy and George over to the closet. "Easy!" Nancy protested. She was worried that if they handled her backpack, they'd feel its odd contents.

Wayne stepped over to a box of mechanics' tools and pulled out two leather straps and two steel clamps. He and Bart joined the girls at the little closet. Wayne opened the door and thrust the girls inside.

Nancy saw that there was a larger hole in the closet wall now. Nearly all the planks had been pried away. It was easy for Wayne to shove the girls through it and into the secret hold.

Switching on a flashlight, Bart grasped Nancy's tied hands with his other hand. Wayne took

George's hands. The two men hustled the girls halfway down the dark hold.

As they approached the middle of the hold, Nancy noticed a huddled shape by one wall. Then Bart's flashlight swung around and lit up the form. Nancy gasped.

Sitting on a stool, his handcuffs chained to rings embedded in the wall, was David Conner!

15

Stick Out Your Tongue . . .

The sight of David Conner anchored so securely to the wall made Nancy realize just how grave their situation was.

Wayne shoved Nancy over to the outside wall of the hold, opposite David. Losing her balance, she lurched backward for a moment. The shoulder straps of her backpack slipped down her arms and jerked against her tied wrists. The backpack with its strange bundle now hung behind her knees.

"What are you going to do with us?" she asked Wayne.

"You might say you're going to become very attached to this ship." Wayne chuckled ghoulishly.

Bart gave George a push across the room. The girls were pushed against a thick iron pipe that ran horizontally along the wall, about three feet

132

up from the floor. Wayne began to wrap a leather strap around Nancy's wrists.

"You don't really expect to get away with this, do you?" Nancy asked him.

"You're just full of questions, aren't you?" Wayne snarled. "You oughta be a reporter like our friend over there. He liked to ask questions, too—and now look. His askin' days are over."

Wayne flashed her a nasty smile. Then he wound the strap around the iron pipe behind her.

"I caught you kids playing around this ship that first night," he added. "I thought the little elevator trick would scare you off. But then there you were the very next night. I figured you needed a stronger message, so I popped you into the river."

Wayne secured the strap to the pipe with the heavy steel clamp, then gave the strap an extra tug. The leather bit cruelly into Nancy's flesh. "And now you're back again," Wayne said. "But this time, you ain't going nowhere."

As Wayne moved over to clamp George to the pipe, Nancy yanked on her strap a few times. She could move her hands and arms a little, but the steel clamp wouldn't budge.

"Come on, Wayne. Faster!" Bart said. He was clearly getting very nervous.

"Do you hear that?" Nancy asked. She nodded toward the ceiling. There was a buzz coming from the room above, and there were other noises—footfalls and clanking china.

"That's people coming to the testimonial din-

133

ner for Clayton," she continued. "They're going to be right above us, and we're expected to be there, too. They'll be looking for us."

"Afraid not, blondie," Wayne said as he finished clamping George's strap. "Everybody's gonna be told that you've been sent on a little errand. By the time they start looking for you, you'll be on your way to the Pacific Ocean."

Wayne made one last check of the bindings. Bart edged nervously back down the hold. Wayne followed him back through the hidden entrance.

Nancy could see the light from the garage hold through the hole. The light grew smaller as the men put the planks back up over the opening.

Nancy, George, and David listened. There seemed to be a problem. Some planks kept clattering back onto the closet floor.

"They must be having trouble getting the planks back up," Nancy whispered. "Those boards have been yanked in and out so often, the nails probably won't stay in place."

After some angry muttering, the two men stopped trying. A few narrow gaps were left where planks had been, and the closet door slammed shut. Nancy, George, and Conner were in total darkness. The only noises were muffled sounds from the dining salon above.

Nancy's eyes began to adjust to the darkness. "David?" she called.

"I'm still here," he answered wryly.

"How did you get in here?" she asked. "I know your specialty as a reporter is dangerous diet plans and scams. Is Clayton manufacturing an illegal diet formula? Is he moving his plant from South America to the Far East?"

David let out a long, low whistle. "How did you figure all that out?"

"It wasn't easy," she said. "Am I right?"

"Yep, I think so," David said. "A good friend of mine almost died using KalorieKill, so I wrote a series of articles that got it banned.

"But then I found out that a new supply had hit the underground market in Europe and the Middle East," he continued. "Just when I had tracked the shipping to San Rafael in Argentina, the plant was closed down and moved out. The *Heartliner* was docked there at the same time, and I thought maybe the crew members had noticed something suspicious. I came here at first just to interview them."

"When did you start to think the *Heartliner* was involved?" Nancy asked.

"When I learned it was the only ship large enough in that area at that time," David answered. "At first I thought Dr. Diaz was involved. He acted so nervous every time I tried to talk to him. I even passed him a note once, bluffing that I knew what was going on. But I didn't put it all together until I realized I was being held prisoner on Clayton's yacht."

"When did they capture you?" Nancy asked.

"Those two thugs caught me snooping around the ship Wednesday night," David said. "I'd called the guard and told him Dr. Diaz wanted him at the hospital. When he left, I boarded ship."

"We followed you on board that night," George said, "but Wayne pushed Nancy overboard."

"I've been tied up on the Clayton yacht ever since," David said. "They moved me here about an hour ago."

"That explains why you weren't here this afternoon," Nancy said, recalling her visit to the hold earlier that day. Then she remembered the tie tack she'd found. It had come in handy as a clue—now it could be a tool to save their lives!

She twisted and turned her arms and her torso. Finally she wriggled the fingers of her right hand down into the pocket of her jeans. With two fingertips, she slowly rolled the tie tack up from the bottom of her pocket. The point of the tack kept pricking her leg, but those little stabs gave her hope that her idea would work.

Finally, Nancy could grasp the tie tack between her thumb and first two fingers. Maneuvering it around, she began poking holes into the leather strap stretched between her wrists and the pipe. Closing her eyes, she tried to place the holes as close together as possible.

"The *Heartliner* leaves tonight, and we're sailing along, I'm afraid," David was saying. "Wayne said he's supposed to plaster over the entrance to the hold so that it won't be inspected during customs checks."

"We'll be plastered in forever?" George said.

"Oh, no," David said. "When they get to the Far East, I was going to be . . . I believe the words 'disposed of' were used. Now that you two are here, I suspect you'll be joining me."

Nancy turned the sharp tack point, twisting it back and forth. She felt the strap getting weaker at the spot she was cutting. At last, it was hanging together now by only a few strands. She stabbed once more, and it broke!

Using both hands, Nancy pushed the broken edge of the leather in and out, unweaving it from around her wrists. Finally she was able to step away from the wall. Her wrists were still tied, but she was free from the pipe.

"Nancy, is that you moving around?" George gasped in surprise.

"Yes, I'm free," Nancy said.

"I don't believe it," David said. "You're part Sherlock Holmes, part Houdini!"

"Not quite," Nancy declared. She felt her way through the dark until she and George were standing back to back. "George, try to untie my

137

hands," she said. She could feel George's fingers fumbling and finally untying Nancy's wrists.

"There, you've got it!" Nancy exclaimed, pulling her hands free. Then she used the tie tack to tear apart George's leather bindings. The job went quickly, now that her hands were untied.

"David, I'm sorry," Nancy said, whipping the twine off of George's wrists. "I can't do anything about your handcuffs or chains. But we'll be back as soon as possible."

"Just don't tell me to 'hang in there,' okay?" David said with a grim chuckle.

Nancy grabbed her backpack, and she and George ran to the end of the hold. Together, they kicked more planks away and climbed through the opening.

They pushed the closet door and picked their way through the dark garage hold. Opening the door, they stepped cautiously into the companionway. There was no sign of Wayne or Bart or anyone else.

The two girls raced up the stairs and headed for the galley. They burst through the door, startling Bess as she stood at a counter arranging fruit cocktail cups on a tray.

"What are you doing here?" Bess cried. "And where have you been? You're a mess!"

Nancy looked down at herself. Her hands were scratched, and her yellow sweater and jeans were streaked with dirt and oil. "We'll tell you later,"

Nancy said, grabbing a white apron. "Right now, we have to catch a criminal."

"What are you two doing here?" Maria echoed just then, coming in from the dining salon.

"Why does everyone keep asking us that?" George said.

"Mr. Clayton said he'd sent you two on a special errand," Bess explained. "He said he'd asked you to go to Chicago to deliver some photos to the newspaper in time for their midnight deadline. I thought maybe you'd solved the case."

"We did," Nancy said, "but Clayton doesn't know it—yet. Maria, please go into the banquet and find Detective Brody and my dad. Ask them to meet George out in the companionway."

Nancy turned to George next. "Fill them in, but don't let Clayton see you. Tell Detective Brody that Wayne and Bart are probably over on Clayton's yacht. He'll need to get some officers there right away." Maria and George hurried out.

"Bess, you come with me," Nancy said, grabbing two large oval trays.

Nancy took out all the papers from her backpack: Jane Firestone's lab reports, the articles about KalorieKill, and copies of the *Heartliner*'s last cruise records. She put them on one tray and covered them with a large napkin.

Then she reached for the dishcloth-wrapped bundle in her backpack. She was surprised at

139

how warm it was. She laid it on the second tray, covered it with a napkin, and handed it to Bess. Angling her arm in the sling carefully, Bess found that she could carry the light tray.

"We're going to surprise Clayton," Nancy told Bess. "You go ahead, and I'll hide behind you—I don't want him to see me yet. Walk straight toward the speakers' table but not too fast. We don't want to attract attention."

Bess stepped into the back of the dining salon, carrying the covered tray in front of her. Nancy walked in a crouch close behind Bess, carrying her own tray with the documents.

In the corner, a mariachi band played lively music. The ceiling was hung with colorful piñatas—hollow papier-mâché animals filled with candy and small toys. Long tables, loaded with serving bowls and platters of tasty South American foods, stretched the length of the room. Large flower arrangements blossomed on each table.

At the far end was the speakers' table, where the mayor and other civic leaders sat, along with Dr. Diaz, Mrs. Diaz, Pepe, and Clayton. They were all wearing formal evening clothes.

Bess stepped slowly, as if walking down an aisle at a wedding. Behind her, Nancy could see around Bess's elbow to the end of her tray.

Nancy's eyes widened. The snowy white napkin on Bess's tray was quivering!

Before Nancy could do anything, the napkin began to jerk around. Then, with a hissing whistle, the bright green head of the lengua fresa popped out from under the linen, flicking its hot pink tongue.

Bess let out a heart-stopping scream and threw the tray into the air!

16

Smooth Sailing Ahead

At the sound of Bess's scream, the elegant banquet turned into a madhouse. Other people screamed, too, even though they didn't know why. Some jumped up in panic and began to run toward the exits.

Meanwhile, Bess's tray flew over two rows of tables like a stainless steel Frisbee and crashed into a pink piñata shaped like a bull. The piñata broke open, showering candy onto the diners below.

The napkin and the dishcloth flew up in the air, too. The dishcloth landed on a nearby table, splashing into Nurse Wells's black bean soup. The napkin fluttered down onto the bald head of one of the guests.

The lengua fresa had the most exciting flight. It landed first in the lap of the bank president's wife. From there it leapt into the strings of the mariachi guitar, then bounced into a lemon flan with a squishy splat. It lay there, its bright tongue lapping at the custard.

Nancy stared at the speakers' table. Alexander Clayton was on his feet, gaping at the lengua fresa. She watched his face change from stunned amazement to disbelief to horror. Finally, with a piercing glare at Nancy, Clayton turned and moved swiftly for the door.

Standing there waiting for him were Dr. Diaz, Detective Brody, and Carson Drew. Quickly Nancy carried the tray of documents to them.

"Alex, my friend," Dr. Diaz said gently, placing a hand on Clayton's shoulder. "It's over."

"Armando!" Clayton said. "I warn you!"

"It's over," Dr. Diaz repeated. "I'm not your puppet anymore." Mrs. Diaz and Maria came to stand next to the doctor, one on each side.

Nancy looked back at Bess, who had collapsed in a nearby chair. George and Pepe were kneeling beside her.

The dining salon was still in chaos. The mayor stepped up to the microphone at the speakers' table. "Ladies and gentlemen," he said, "please, please. Let's all be calm."

As he looked down at the table, the lengua fresa gazed up at him, a little lemon flan dripping down its chin. The mayor put his hand over the microphone and muttered, "Will someone please get that thing out of here!"

Pepe came up quickly and took the lizard by its

front legs. Holding it firmly, he walked through the dining salon back to the kitchen. Some people made faces as he passed. Everyone stepped back and gave him plenty of room.

"Let's go someplace quiet," Detective Brody said as he took hold of Clayton's arm.

"The library," Dr. Diaz suggested, leading the way.

"Nancy, you come, too," Detective Brody said. "George said you have some documents for me."

Detective Brody, Clayton, the Diaz family, Nancy, and Mr. Drew went to the library. Before they had sat down, Manuel came to the door. Behind him, three police officers escorted in Wayne and Bart, who were both in handcuffs.

Detective Brody turned to Nancy. "Are these the men who kidnapped you and George?" he asked.

"They certainly are," she answered. "And David Conner's still down in the hold. I'll bet Wayne has the keys to unlock David's handcuffs."

One of the officers reached for a large ring of keys clipped onto Wayne's belt. "I'll take these and try them until I find which one works," he offered. Nancy gave him a copy of the ship diagram and showed him where David Conner was chained, and the officer left. Detective Brody asked Manuel to go get Pepe, Bess, and George and have them bring down the lenguas fresas.

Then Nancy briefed the others on what she'd

found below in the two cargo holds. "I knew we were looking for something large and heavy, because of the different weight figures on the two sets of cruise records Maria found," Nancy said.

"I'm sorry we snooped in your study, Dad," Maria put in. "I was just so worried."

"It's all right, Maria. Those records were also my first clue that something was wrong," Dr. Diaz admitted. "These are records we prepare for the U.S. authorities when we return to home port. I was wondering why the ship's weight was so high. Then Alexander destroyed my original set of papers and substituted a set of false declarations."

Dr. Diaz sank down into a chair. "I couldn't figure out why he faked those papers. Then I got to wondering why he had fired our crew in San Rafael and hired a new crew of locals. I went down to the cargo hold and found the machinery. That's when I confronted Alex."

"Armando! I'm warning you!" Clayton thundered, his face growing red.

"No more, Alex," Armando said. He sat back in his chair and closed his eyes. "No more warnings, no more blackmail." He opened his eyes and looked at Nancy, continuing, "I argued with him for hours, but he refused to listen. He was determined to continue his plan."

"To move the diet formula plant?" Nancy asked. She told the others how Clayton had dismantled his factory and stored it on the *Heartliner*. She showed Jane Firestone's findings to Detective Brody. "We think he intended to relocate the plant in the Far East," she concluded.

"Sri Lanka," Dr. Diaz agreed. "I wanted to tell the authorities, but—" He hesitated. "Alexander knows something about my past. It's something that even you don't know, Francesca."

Watching Dr. Diaz hang his head, Nancy felt sorry for him. "I know now that I should never have kept such a secret," he added in a subdued voice. "It was a very dangerous thing to do."

Mrs. Diaz took his hand. "Whatever it is, Armando, it will be all right," she told him loyally. "I'll stand by you always." Nancy moved to Maria's side and put her arm around her friend's shoulders.

Clasping his wife's hand, Dr. Diaz swallowed and went on with his story. "When we got back to the States, I decided to tell the police, no matter what the consequences would be. I gathered the papers I needed. Then I called Alex to tell him that I was going to the authorities. After all, he was my friend, and I wanted to warn him."

He shook his head heavily. "It was then that I discovered how desperate Alex really was," the doctor went on. "He sent two men to my house— those two, Detective." He waved his hand toward Bart and Wayne.

146

"Monday night, when Maria and I found you?" Nancy asked. "When you said you had fallen?"

"Yes," Dr. Diaz admitted. "Alexander's men hit me. But even worse, they threatened to hurt my family and the children who would be visiting the *Heartliner.* And bad things *were* happening —the awful gas was released in the dining salon, the bed chains broke, and then the needles in ICU were tampered with. I tried so hard to prevent the accidents—that's why I stepped in to draw your blood that afternoon, Nancy, so that nothing more would go wrong."

"Did you check the basket of needles?" Nancy asked.

"Yes." He sighed. "Pepe was right—there was venom from the barba amarilla on them. I was planning to take them to the police as soon as I had told my family about my past."

"Not all those incidents were caused by Clayton," Mr. Drew noted. "The noxious gas was released by Sara Lawson."

"Yes, but she did it because Alex forced me to fire her," Dr. Diaz pointed out. "And I'm sure Alexander did those other things just to show me that he would stop at nothing."

"You have no proof," Clayton said tightly, his eyes narrowed to slits.

Bart cleared his throat. "Officer, Wayne and I did that stuff—we cut the bed chains and put poison on the needles. Mr. Clayton told us to."

"You fool!" Clayton yelled at Bart. Then he swiveled to face Detective Brody. "This is absurd. I demand to see my attorney."

"You can call him from downtown," Detective Brody assured him. The two waiting officers led Wayne, Bart, and Clayton out the door.

"Why would a successful businessman like Alexander Clayton get mixed up in something so bad?" Nancy wondered aloud when the door had shut behind them.

Dr. Diaz shrugged. "I knew that his business was in trouble a while back," he said. "He put a good face on it, but I guess he was desperate for a new source of income. Alex couldn't give up the trappings of wealth—the yacht, the mansion, the status in the community. KalorieKill must have made him a load of money, even after it was banned."

Suddenly there was a slight commotion at the door. It opened and Bess, George, and Pepe entered. Pepe carried the lengua fresa in a bucket.

Crinkling her nose, Bess peered into the bucket. "Nancy, tell me one thing," she asked. "Why was this creature in the refrigerator on Clayton's yacht?"

"When the ammonium sulfide was released on Monday," Dr. Diaz said, "Clayton ran down to the hold to check that the lizards weren't poisoned."

148

"So that's who I saw running down to the lower deck that day!" Nancy realized, snapping her fingers.

Dr. Diaz nodded. "He later came to me and showed me this one lengua fresa he'd found lying on its back. He was very nervous, and he wanted me to perform an autopsy. I said no—I'm not a herpetologist."

"A what?" Bess asked.

"A reptile doctor," Dr. Diaz translated. "Anyway, Clayton was afraid the lizards would all die, and he'd have no more raw material for his diet powder. I guess he was keeping this one until he could find a herpetologist. The cold in the refrigerator probably kept it comatose."

"Well, the little critter sure recovered when it got warmed up!" Bess said, making a face. They all laughed as they remembered the scene in the dining salon.

"I had to go along with the dinner tonight," Dr. Diaz explained when the laughter died down. "I couldn't let Alexander know what I had in mind. I planned to talk to Francesca and Maria after the dinner—and you, too, Pepe. Then I was going to take the poisoned needles, the papers, and my story to the police tomorrow morning."

"It's true. He'd made an appointment to talk with me tomorrow morning," Detective Brody said.

"It was almost too late." Dr. Diaz sighed.

"Nancy, I'm so sorry for the danger you, George, and Mr. Conner were in this evening. If only I had come forward sooner . . ."

Nancy drew a deep breath as she remembered how close she had come to being abducted.

"Detective Brody, I'll gather my evidence and come to the police station shortly to give you a formal statement," Dr. Diaz said. He put his arm around Maria. Nancy saw a new expression on his face. The sadness and the fear had been replaced with courage and determination.

Just then the other police officer returned with David Conner, freed from the cargo hold. "We checked the machinery hold across the hall—Wayne's key ring had the key to the new lock," Conner said. "The lizards were all crammed in there, as well as the cans of KalorieKill. Clayton must have realized you were getting too close, Nancy, and he moved the little rascals."

"Speaking of moving, we ought to move on home ourselves," Carson Drew put in. "It sounds as if all the other dinner guests have been ushered off the ship by now. This will certainly be one banquet they'll never forget!"

"I say we have another testimonial dinner tomorrow night," Bess said. "Only this one should be for Nancy Drew!" Everyone agreed and congratulated Nancy.

"I say it's time to order pizza," Nancy quickly changed the subject. "I missed most of the banquet, remember? What kind shall we order,

Bess? After what we've learned this week, you're not staying on a starvation diet, I hope."

"Nope," Bess said. "I'll have an order of pasta with veggie sauce and a small salad with diet dressing. I'm giving up crash diets for good, thanks to you, Nancy!"

2314